THE GAME
DON'T CHANGE

MAZARADI FOX
WITH BRITTANI WILLIAMS

Infamous

This is a work of fiction. All names, characters, places, and incidents are a product of the author's imagination. Any resemblance to real events or persons, living or dead, is entirely coincidental.

Published by Akashic Books
©2016 Estate of Mazaradi Fox

ISBN: 978-1-61775-482-1
Library of Congress Control Number: 2016935166
All rights reserved

First printing

Infamous Books
www.infamousbooks.net

Akashic Books
Twitter: @AkashicBooks
Facebook: AkashicBooks
E-mail: info@akashicbooks.com
Website: www.akashicbooks.com

Also Available from Infamous Books

Caught Up
by Shannon Holmes

The White House
by JaQuavis Coleman

Black Lotus
by K'wan

Swing
by Miasha

H.N.I.C.
by Albert "Prodigy" Johnson with Steven Savile

Sunfail
by Steven Savile

The game don't change . . . the players do . . .

Jamal Green, a.k.a. Mazaradi Fox, wrote this fictional story in 2013 during his incarceration at the Orleans Correctional Facility in Albion, New York. The harsh realities he experienced inspired this work. During the last years of his life, his mind, body, and spirit began to change as he reaffirmed his faith in God. His renewed focus was on the future for all of those around him, especially the youth. He wanted more for them than he had given himself; it was his goal for the next generation to learn from his mistakes instead of being doomed to repeat them. May his untimely death be a lesson to us all, and may he rest in eternal peace as his legacy lives on.

CHAPTER ONE

"Mr. DeMarco Jones, I hereby sentence you to eighteen months at the Tryon Residential Center for your role in the robbery in question. You will remain in custody until the end of the eighteen-month term."

As the judge spoke, DeMarco was off in his own world. He immediately began to think about all the time he was set to serve. For a teenager, eighteen months was an eternity. He wasn't mentally prepared to be away from the streets of Queens and his friends for that long.

"Fuck," he said under his breath.

"What was that, Mr. Jones?" the judge spoke in a deep baritone. He had the kind of voice that vibrated through you. There was no question that when he spoke, he meant business.

"Uh, nothing, Your Honor. I ain't say nothin ," De-Marco said, sitting there next to his lawyer who didn't do shit for him.

"In closing, I hope you learn your lesson from this

situation and make the best of it. You still have time to turn your life around, young man. Court is dismissed," the judge said and banged his gavel.

Man, I see already I ain't gonna like this shit, DeMarco was thinking to himself as he sat in a van with ten other kids on their way to Tryon. He was already contemplating ways to get out of the situation. He was imagining multiple routes to escape without even knowing the layout of the detention center. For the first time in his life, he felt like he didn't have control and it was uncomfortable. He was used to doing things his way without being a "yes" man. This would be his first time locked away, but many of his friends had endured the same fate. From their experiences, he learned that you could do one of two things: sink or swim. Sinking was just not an option for him.

Man, the first chance I get I'm up outta here, he thought to himself. He was getting more annoyed by the minute as the kids around him started playing the tough-guy role. He sat quietly in deep thought waiting for someone to get out of line with him. He was always ready to knock a nigga on his ass if necessary. Finally, they pulled off the road and passed a sign that said, *Welcome to Tryon Residential Center for Boys.* Taking a deep breath, DeMarco stilled himself as he got out of the van.

"Grab your bags and follow me," the driver said as he walked toward a door that read, *Intake.* Once at the door, the staffer held it open for the young men. DeMarco walked inside with his three bags and couldn't believe that he was going to have to stay there for the next eighteen months. The guards stared each of the boys up and down, clearly trying to intimidate them. Some young men buckled at the knees, but DeMarco kept a straight face.

"Put your bags against that wall and then follow me," one guard said to the group as he walked down the hall. "Now take a seat."

Each of them found a spot and did as they were told.

"After you see the nurse, go across the hall and someone will give you a card with the cottage name on it. Once that's done, come back up the hall and I'll send you on your way."

Man, this is some bullshit, DeMarco thought as he sat there waiting for his name to be called. All sorts of ideas flooded his mind as he looked around the room studying the other boys. He watched their movements carefully. He was taught not to trust anyone, not even your best friend. He was also taught to be ready at all times in the event an enemy attacked. He sat impatiently for the next fifteen minutes until his name was called.

"Jones!"

"About time," he mumbled under his breath.

"What's that?" the guard asked.

"I ain't say nothin," DeMarco replied.

DeMarco headed into the nurse's office with a straight face. After about twenty minutes of bullshit, he walked across the hall to find out what cottage he was going to be in. He grabbed the card off the desk, turned, and stepped back out of the office.

"Ya card," a guard said.

DeMarco handed it to him.

"Elmwood One. Oh, that's Mrs. B. I think you'll like it there. When you go out of the door, turn right and follow the road. It will be the second cottage on your right side. Just give her this card and she'll handle everything from there."

At that point DeMarco didn't give a fuck what cottage he was in or who the staff members were. All he wanted to do was get there and get to his bed. A couple minutes later he walked through the door of his new home. It wasn't sweet, but he would have no choice other than making the best out of it.

"You must be Mr. Jones," a chubby guy said.

"Last time I checked," DeMarco answered.

"A funny guy, I see. I have just the place for you: room five. You go down the hall, make a left, and you'll find it. By the way, my name is Mr. Johnson."

Not saying shit, DeMarco just grabbed his bags and followed the directions. Reading the numbers on the door, DeMarco found his room and went in.

You can't be serious, he thought as he looked around the two-man room, seeing how dirty it was. He didn't have the energy to do anything but make his bed. DeMarco slipped under the covers and fell right to sleep, missing the block already.

What the fuck? DeMarco said to himself when he was awakened by nearby voices. Sitting up, he noticed three white boys sitting on the bed across the room. Mad as hell that they'd woken him up, he grabbed his toothpaste, toothbrush, washcloth, and walked out of the room. Ten minutes later DeMarco came back into his room and saw the same people sitting on the bed. Putting his stuff down on the top of the locker at the foot of his bed, DeMarco turned to the dudes across the room.

"Ayo, which one of y'all sleep in here?" he asked, standing up, hoping that one of them would get smart.

"I do," the one in the middle said.

"A'ight, so you and you," he said, pointing at the other two. "Y'all got to go. All that early-morning hanging-out shit, talking loud—that shit is a wrap."

"Lil' Nicky, you hear this fucking kid?" the one on the right said, laughing.

Not thinking twice, DeMarco walked over and punched him in the mouth. Blood splattered and his lip immediately began to swell.

"Now laugh at that, pussy-ass white boy, on your way out my fucking room," DeMarco said as he stepped back.

Both of them left, looking scared, one of them holding his mouth.

"Now look, Lil' Nicky, or whatever your name is. First thing is, you gonna clean this dirty-ass shit up," De-Marco said as he started unpacking his bags. "And all that throwing your clothes all over the place, that shit is a wrap too. Fuck I look like? I'm not sleeping in dirt. Next thing: this is my side and that's your side of the room. If I catch any one of your lil' buddies on my side of the room, or if anything goes missing because you got nig-gas coming in and out, I'm holding you responsible. You got me?"

Lil' Nicky, just as scared as his friends, nodded his head. DeMarco had him just where he wanted him.

After pulling out his favorite rap posters from his bags, DeMarco began to hang them up. The posters—which he had gotten from *The Source* magazine—were of Nas, Tupac, Lil' Kim, Biggie, Mobb Deep, Da Brat, Run-D.M.C., and some others. In the middle of putting his clothes in his locker, the staff yelled out that it was lunchtime.

"Ayo, where we go to eat lunch?" he asked.

"On weekends we eat every meal here, but Monday through Friday we eat breakfast and lunch in the cafeteria and dinner in here," Lil' Nicky explained.

"A'ight, cool," DeMarco said, and walked out of the room.

After lunch, DeMarco was sitting in his room writing a letter home when Lil' Nicky came in and told him that the counselor wanted to see him. DeMarco put his letter down and stood up, about to head out of the room to find the counselor. Lil' Nicky dropped and began doing push-ups.

"Now that's what the fuck I'm talkin about. How many sets you got in?" DeMarco asked as he pulled off the shirt from over his wifebeater, deciding the counselor could come find him if it was so important.

"This is the third one. Thirty a clip," Lil' Nicky said once he got up.

"A'ight, bet, let me catch up real quick," DeMarco said, quickly knocking out the ninety push-ups in two sets. The two were so caught up in their workout that neither of them realized how fast the time had flown by. After twenty more minutes of push-ups and sit-ups, De-Marco laid back on his bed with his eyes closed to calm himself down.

"Nicky, I know this room better be clean!" a female voice yelled.

DeMarco opened his eyes, but had to close them again because he thought he was bugging out. When he blinked again she was gone. Sitting up, he looked over at Lil' Nicky and asked, "Ayo, who was that?"

As he sat up on his bed laughing, Lil' Nicky said, "That's Mrs. B. Yo, I'm telling you, she's the baddest female on the compound."

"Yo, I thought that was Stacey Dash standing in the doorway. Man, I got to go check on her even though she a little too short for me," DeMarco said as he got up, grabbing his shirt and leaving the room.

Walking down the hall he saw Mrs. B sitting at the staff desk in the walkway. He had to admit she was bad as fuck. She had a fat ass and curves for days. He watched her movements imagining how she'd look naked. He'd been with a few older women, but none as fine as her. It was now his mission to get a piece of Mrs. B.

Stepping to the bathroom he heard, "So, you must be Jones."

He turned to her and said, "Yup, I guess that's me."

He kept walking into the shower room. He didn't want to seem pressed; he wanted her to make the first move.

* * *

For the next couple of weeks—after their brief encounter in the hall—Mrs. B made it her business to frequently stop by his room. Every time she came he acted as if she wasn't there. He could tell that she was feeling him and he was figuring out a way that it could work to his advantage. Getting pussy would be a plus, but getting her to help him get out of there would be even better.

"Man, I'm telling you, DeMarco, Mrs. B feeling you, yo. She ain't never stopped by my room until you got here," Lil' Nicky said while the two were working out.

"Man, fuck shorty, yo. I'm focused on going home," DeMarco replied as he dropped down to do his set, all the while thinking of a master plan. He wasn't comfortable enough to tell Nicky what was on his mind, but fucking Mrs. B was definitely part of the plan.

Five months went by so fast that DeMarco didn't realize it until his birthday came and went. By then he and Lil' Nicky had grown pretty tight. He also found himself flirting with Mrs. B more and more, to the point where he would ask her to do her hair in a particular style or to wear certain clothes. She would always do it. Mrs. B saw how all the quiet guys gravitated toward him—even trying to talk and dress like him. The young thug that had all the other boys in check turned her on.

"Ayo, I don't give a fuck, Reek. You ain't gonna keep tryna play me. Just 'cause you from the city, that don't mean shit to me!" DeMarco heard Lil' Nicky saying one night as he was walking by the bathroom. Wanting to see if Lil' Nicky was a soft upstate nigga or if he had bust a hammer before, DeMarco kept it moving to his room. A couple minutes later, Lil' Nicky came in with his face red as fuck and tight.

"That pussy-ass nigga Reek think I'm soft or somethin 'cause I'm not from the city. I guess I'ma have to show him how we get down upstate," Lil' Nicky said out loud to himself, as DeMarco sat on his bed acting like he wasn't listening. "Wait till Mrs. B come on. I know these niggas gonna try to jump me, but I don't give a fuck. I'm gonna knock all his teeth out his mouth. Watch!"

DeMarco drifted off to sleep but woke up when he heard Mrs. B at his door.

"Wassup, lil' DeMarco?"

"Ain't nothing little about me, Mrs. B," DeMarco replied with a devilish grin.

She had on a tight pair of white jeans with a fitted shirt. Just seeing her standing in the doorway made his dick hard. He wanted to jump on her right there at that moment, but he held his composure.

"So you say," Mrs. B said, smiling as she walked away.

DeMarco slipped his feet into his sneakers, grabbed his toothbrush, and headed out of the room. Walking into the bathroom, he saw Lil' Nicky talking to Mrs. B and thought to himself, *I knew that nigga was soft!* All he could do was shake his head. He wasn't mad at Lil' Nicky, just a little let down. After handling his business, DeMarco returned to his room and found Lil' Nicky sitting on his bed.

"What's poppin, Lil' Nicky?"

"Shit. You? Today I ain't gonna work out; you feel me?"

"Yeah, I was gonna take today off anyway to rest," DeMarco said, placing his things in his locker before leaving the room again.

Sitting in the dayroom playing cards with a few dudes who looked up to him, DeMarco heard Reek over in the TV room with his crew. He could tell that none of Reek's crew was tough unless they were in a group. As he continued playing cards he noticed Lil' Nicky approach the dayroom doorway and stop, then look around a few times and head toward the TV room. Seeing this, De-Marco put his cards down and got up from the table, moving slowly toward the TV room. Not knowing if Lil' Nicky was going to do something, DeMarco didn't want him to feel that he was by himself and Reek had a crew of dudes with him. When he made it to the TV room doorway, DeMarco watched Lil' Nicky walk slowly to the front of the room where Reek was sitting.

"I'm told you been talkin shit about me, bitch," De-Marco heard Lil' Nicky say before he started raining blows on Reek.

Everybody was so shocked that it took his boys a moment to realize what was going on. By this time DeMarco slid closer to Reek's man who was nearest to Lil' Nicky. As soon as the guy stood up to move on Lil' Nicky, De-Marco leveled him, causing all kinds of ruckus as the TV room erupted into an all-out fight. DeMarco, Lil' Nicky, and the "Quiet Boys"—as they called themselves—were pitted against the city crew. When Mrs. B and the other staff members ran up front, they couldn't believe what they were seeing. It reminded Mrs. B of a royal rumble. There were muthafuckers fighting everywhere. As Lil' Nicky and DeMarco were kicking someone on the ground, Mrs. B waited, and then pulled the pin on her radio.

Three minutes later, everyone was lying on the floor.

"DeMarco, you snake bitch, you supposed to be from the city!" one of the dudes shouted.

"Nigga, I'm my own man!" DeMarco said, laughing. "Plus, I'm from southside Jamaica, Queens. Remember that!"

After what seemed like two hours lying on the floor, Mrs. B came back with five staff members and started pointing at people. DeMarco knew they were in deep shit, but at that moment, he didn't even care. Lil' Nicky was his boy and he vowed to have his back.

The staff was yelling for everyone to get up from the floor; there was a lot of commotion. Obscenities were being flung and threats were being made. DeMarco noticed Lil' Nicky staring at him while the guards were escorting people out of the TV room.

"That was some real shit, DeMarco. I'll never forget that," Lil' Nicky said. From the look on his face, DeMarco could tell that he meant it from the heart.

"Ain't shit, Nick. I told you before I'd always have your back," DeMarco replied as he headed out and found Mrs. B sitting at her desk.

"You wanna tell me what the fuck that was all about?" she said, tapping her foot.

"They tried to play my boy, and when he didn't back down, they tried to jump him," DeMarco said, looking Mrs. B directly in the eyes. "I wasn't just gonna stand there and let that happen. Loyalty is one of the most important things to me in life and I'm loyal to those who are loyal to me. Point blank."

"You and that fuckin Costolow. We'll see how fuckin loyal y'all are to each other when his ass is on the line. Just go to your room!" Mrs. B snapped. "Send Costolow back here."

DeMarco was pissed about the way she was talking to him, but instead of making another scene he just went into his room. He lay back on his bed and closed his eyes, thinking about the streets that he missed so much.

CHAPTER TWO

For the next couple days, Mrs. B was running down hard on Lil' Nicky and DeMarco. Obviously punishment for the melee; they were practically slaves. Every time there was something that needed to be cleaned, she used both of them and DeMarco always got the brunt of the work.

"Ayo, Lil' Nicky, I'm tellin you, I'm about to ask Mrs. B wassup wit her," DeMarco said one night as he and Lil' Nicky chilled in their room. "Yo, she been on us hard these last couple days."

"Who you tellin? It's like every time she's here, she doesn't know any other name but ours," Lil' Nicky replied. "She be on your back the most though. I don't know what the fuck you said to her, but you definitely pissed her off."

Just then a guard yelled, "Okay, lights out!"

"Damn, it's 11 already?" DeMarco said, looking at his watch. "I'm tellin you, if she comes to work tomorrow, I'm gonna tell her about herself."

DeMarco lay there silent. In his head he was working on his lines as if he was an actor preparing for a role. He knew he had to step to her correctly or he'd end up cleaning more shit. Wanting to be sure everybody was asleep, he planned to wait until around 2:30 before even thinking about pressing Mrs. B. He knew she was feeling him; that was a given. What he didn't understand was why she was on him so hard. The time passed quickly and soon it was going on 1:30. To his surprise, Mrs. B seemed to have the same idea.

"I want to talk to you," she said, shining her flashlight on him, then she turned and walked away, leaving the door open.

DeMarco slipped on a pair of sneakers and walked out of the room, not even thinking to put on a shirt. While coming down the hall he saw that Mrs. B wasn't sitting at her desk. Turning the corner and heading up front, he noticed that the back door to the staff office was open. He went over and peeked his head in.

"Mrs. B," he called in.

"Come in," she said.

He walked into the office to find Mrs. B leaning against the table by the refrigerator.

"Wassup, Mrs. B?"

She walked over to where DeMarco was standing and closed the door.

"You know what I had to go through to keep you here, after the little stunt you and your boy pulled?" Mrs. B stared at him. "I'm so angry with your little ass, I just wanna punch you myself!"

"My fault, Mrs. B. I was just looking out for my boy," DeMarco said, leaning up against the wall. "I wasn't tryna cause you no trouble. And you keep callin me *little* but I keep tellin you ain't nothin little about me."

"We'll see about that," Mrs. B said as she cased the room.

Standing in front of him now, she stuck her hand down his shorts, grabbed his dick, and started rubbing it. Shocked at first, he just stood there. Then, coming out of his daze, he pulled Mrs. B into him and grabbed her ass.

"So far so good," she said as she pulled his dick out. She dropped to her knees and wrapped her lips around his dick, almost causing him to moan out loud as she slid him all the way down her throat.

"Damn," he said, glancing down. He had to admit: the way she was looking at him while sucking his dick was driving him crazy. Getting up, Mrs. B took a few steps back and started stepping out of her clothes while keeping her eyes fixed on him.

"You sure you can handle this?" she asked. "This ain't that little-girl pussy you used to."

"And I ain't them old-ass limp-dick niggas you used to," he said with confidence, though in truth he was a little nervous.

He knew that whatever happened right now, he had to hold his own: no ifs, ands, or buts about it. Mrs. B stood butt-ass naked in front of him. His eyes roamed all over her body. She was thick as hell with all the right curves. She was right about one thing: she wasn't like any young chick he'd ever had. She was *all* woman.

"Gotdamn, Mrs. B," he said as he continued to stare at her. Even though he wasn't really into mixed looking chicks, he had to admit Mrs. B had one of the best bodies he'd ever seen. "All that's mine?"

"If you can handle it," she said, smiling at him.

"Bend ova the table," he instructed.

He walked up on her, sticking two fingers inside of her. She immediately moaned loudly. It was the confidence booster he needed as he grabbed her ponytail with one hand and used the other to aim his dick. Sliding up in her, he couldn't hold his own moan in this time. She was super wet and tight as hell.

As he slowly moved in and out of her, Mrs. B looked over her shoulder and said, "If you can't handle it, I'll understand."

Hearing her say that, all nervousness, fear, or whatever was holding him back evaporated. "Oh, I can handle it," he said, and started digging deeper into her.

He had a point to prove now. He wanted to show her that he could not only handle her, but also be the best she'd ever had. He was stroking her up and down and from left to right. Every so often, he'd pull almost all the way out, then thrust into her harder. Her moans grew louder and louder.

"Lay down on the floor," he said as he pulled out of her.

He was taking full control and she obeyed his every command. Getting down on the ground, he put a leg on each of his shoulders and slid back inside of her. He moved in and out of her slowly at first. He pushed her legs back as far as they could go, leading him into a push-up position.

"Give it to me hard," she said.

That was all he needed to hear. He started pounding her pussy with force, causing her to yell out all kinds of sounds. That only made him go harder, and they went like that for the next forty-five minutes. They fucked in every possible position with her doing shit to him no chick had ever done.

"Damn, baby, yesssss, yessss, fuck me! Oh my god. Not right there! How you find that spot? Ohh, I'mmmmmm about to cummmmm!" she yelled out.

Those words made him bust inside of her. He fell on top of her, both of them breathing heavily. He rolled onto his back and was shocked when she took him into her mouth again.

"Just wanna make sure I got it all," she said.

His mind was blown, but he wasn't sprung. This encounter with Mrs. B was necessary if he was going to get out of there before his full sentence was served.

For the next couple of days, Mrs. B worked the graveyard shift, 11 p.m. to 7 a.m. Once everyone was asleep, she would get him from his room and they would fuck like rabbits.

"I think I'm falling in love with ya young ass," Mrs. B said one night as they lay catching their breath.

"Nah, you don't love me, you just love the pipe game," DeMarco replied, rubbing on her titties.

"Yeah, I love that part too," Mrs. B said, and straddled him. "But I am really falling for you." She was rubbing her pussy on his shaft to get his dick hard again. She was ready for round two.

Sliding down on his dick, Mrs. B planned on going until they couldn't anymore—this was her last overnight shift for the next two months.

With each passing day, DeMarco grew more tired of the detention center. He was suffering from a severe case of cabin fever. He hadn't figured out how he could escape, but it was all he could think about. There was nothing more important to him than returning to the streets. This stay was supposed to rehabilitate him, but it was doing the complete opposite: it would only make him hit the streets even harder than before.

"Man, I'm tired of this fuckin place," Lil' Nicky said as he and DeMarco worked out.

"So bounce then," DeMarco responded, laughing, and walked out of the room.

"If you're going outside, go now," Mrs. B said when she noticed him in the hall.

"I'll pass, Mrs. B. I'm chillin inside today," he replied. "I got a couple letters to write that I shoulda written already."

About fifteen minutes later, Mrs. B was calling De-Marco's name.

"Ayo, wassup, Mrs. B?" DeMarco said, sticking his head out the door.

She waved him down the hall and DeMarco went to

see what she wanted. After a few minutes of talking with her, DeMarco returned to his room.

"Ayo, Lil' Nicky," DeMarco said, "you my man, right? I can trust you?"

Sitting up in his bed, Lil' Nicky looked at DeMarco like he was crazy. "Of course you can trust me. Wassup?"

"I'm about to do something and I need you to hold me down," DeMarco said.

"Man, I got you."

"A'ight, I need you to go stand in the rec room and watch out for everybody outside," DeMarco said. "If you see anybody about to come inside, make mad noise."

"When?"

"Right now!"

"So you ain't gon' tell me what the hell is happenin?"

"If I told you, I'd have to kill you." DeMarco laughed.

Lil' Nicky shook his head as he headed over to the rec room. DeMarco followed him closely. A few seconds later, he slid through the back door to the staff office where Mrs. B waited for him. When she saw him, she pulled down her sweatpants and bent over right in the middle of the office.

"Now get on ya hands and knees," DeMarco said. Mrs. B did as told.

Kneeling behind her, DeMarco knew they didn't have much time, but he had to lick her pretty-ass pussy real quick; he just couldn't help it. After a few minutes of pleasing her with his tongue, DeMarco slid inside of her from behind, loving the way her pussy gripped his dick.

"What the fuck?" Lil' Nicky said as he heard moans

coming from the staff office. He went around to the door to see what the hell was going on and noticed that it was open a little. He couldn't believe what he was seeing when he pushed the door a bit. DeMarco was blowing Mrs. B's back out in the doggy-style position. Creeping away from the door, he returned to the rec room smiling.

I knew that nigga was fucking Mrs. B! Lil' Nicky thought to himself as he continued to play lookout.

CHAPTER THREE

"Ayo, Lil' Nicky. You sleep over there?" DeMarco asked.

"No, I'm tryna figure out why the fuck you sittin up at 12:30 at night dressed in all black," Lil' Nicky said as he sat up.

DeMarco had been planning this night for the last two weeks. At first he didn't know if Mrs. B would do it or not, but he tried his hand with her anyway, and to his surprise she said yes. The plan was for Mrs. B to leave the door unlocked when she finished her shift at 11. She really didn't want him to leave, but he promised her he'd call her as soon as he was free and he vowed to keep her name out of it.

"Nigga, I'm about to bounce. That's why I'm dressed in all black," DeMarco said, glancing at his watch.

"I don't know how you gonna do that with all the doors locked," Lil' Nicky replied.

"Man, fuck all that shit, you stayin or you goin? It's

up to you." DeMarco got up and began pacing the room. "I'll tell you this: once that phone rings, I'm gone."

Lil' Nicky was surprised. He wasn't prepared to make a run for it. He wondered if DeMarco had thought everything out carefully because he wasn't trying to do any more time than he had to. After a few seconds of contemplating, Nicky decided that he wasn't about to be left behind. He jumped out of the bed, grabbed the darkest clothes he had, and pulled them on along with his black Nikes.

"Nigga, you know I'm in," Lil' Nicky said just as they heard the phone ring.

DeMarco peeked out of the door and saw the guard get up to answer the call. "Let's go," he said. He didn't know how long the guard was going to stay on the phone, so they had to move quickly. Once the two of them were outside that door, they were going to run like their lives depended on it—because it did. Moving up the hallway, DeMarco put his hand on the doorknob to open it when he heard someone yell, "What the hell are y'all doing over there?"

DeMarco shoved the door open and took flight with Lil' Nicky right behind him.

"He's calling it in!" Lil' Nicky yelled.

"So what? Fuck 'em. They gotta catch us now!" DeMarco said as they flew by the intake office, making their way out of the building.

"Once we hit these woods, they won't be able to drive and see us!" DeMarco said loud enough, so Lil' Nicky could hear him.

"Man, you hear all them cop cars already?" Lil' Nicky was scared shitless. In a million years he would've never had the guts to escape on his own.

"Yeah, I hear it, nigga; just keep moving. We gotta make it to the other side of the road." DeMarco kneeled down with Lil' Nicky between some bushes.

"Let's make it then," Lil' Nicky replied, and they got ready to jump.

DeMarco took a deep breath and said, "A'ight, let's move."

As they came out of the bushes and hit the road, a cop car appeared out of nowhere, almost swiping them.

Errrrrrrr! was all that was heard as they hit the other side of the street and headed into the woods..

"Damn, it feels like we've been running for months," Lil' Nicky said when they cut through a cluster of trees and noticed some bright lights.

Finally, DeMarco spotted the Mobil gas station that Mrs. B told him to be on the lookout for. He was trying to figure out how the fuck they could make it across the road without being run over. Just then, a jeep pulled up to the gas station and parked beside the pump closest to the road. A woman exited the vehicle and left it empty with the engine running while she went inside. DeMarco saw this as their chance.

"Come on!" he barked, and flew across the road, making his way to the jeep while watching the gas station doors. He was about to pull open the driver's-side door when the woman walked out. "Fuck!" He played it off and walked past the jeep as if he was going into the gas station, then headed back over to Lil' Nicky. A couple of minutes later a black Ford truck drove up into the same spot the woman had just pulled out of. Leaving his truck running, the driver went into the store, and DeMarco made his move again.

"Get in!" DeMarco called out as he jumped in the truck. DeMarco pulled away before Lil' Nicky could even close the door.

DeMarco knew how to drive, but with his adrenaline pumping, he was swerving in and out of lanes. Lil' Nicky was so scared he asked him to slow down a few times.

Eventually Lil' Nicky dozed off while DeMarco rapped along with the songs that played on the radio. After a couple hours of driving, they began to see signs indicating they were approaching New York City. DeMarco felt relieved to be so close to home. As he pulled up to a tollbooth, nervousness set in. He hadn't thought that they needed money to get into the city. They couldn't risk going through without paying and getting pulled over by the cops.

"Nicky, get up! We gotta figure out how we gonna pay for this toll."

Lil' Nicky jolted awake in a state of confusion. "What's goin on?"

"Man, look and see if he left any money layin around in here," DeMarco said.

Lil' Nicky, now focused, went through the glove box and every other place he could think to look. He didn't find even a penny. Not knowing where else to search,

DeMarco pulled out the ashtray in frustration and saw that it was full of quarters.

"Got it!" He let out a sigh of relief.

The relief was short-lived when he rolled up to the tollbooth.

"Ticket," the chick at the window said.

Fuck, DeMarco thought. "Gimme a second," he said, and began to look around for a ticket he knew he didn't have.

Nicky joined in too, acting like he was searching as well. The woman was visibly annoyed as a line of cars formed behind them.

"What if I can't find it?" DeMarco asked. "I must've threw it out by accident at the rest stop."

"Then you gotta pay from the free spot," she replied with an attitude.

"A'ight then, how much is that?"

"$6.80," she said.

Under any other circumstance he would've cursed her out for her tone, but he was trying to stay under the radar. He looked over at Nicky who was counting out the change from the ashtray.

"Got it!" Lil' Nicky said.

DeMarco was able to relax again and take a deep breath. He quickly passed her the change and pulled off smiling as they headed toward Grand Central. "Home sweet home!" he yelled.

Turning onto Merrick Boulevard, DeMarco could tell that not much had changed. He drove up the block slowly, looking around, and all he could do was smile.

"Ayo, look, Lil' Nicky, I know you wanna go holla at ya peoples, so let's get a few dollars and I'll leave you with the whip," he said as he pulled over. "You can drive it if you want, but remember, it's hot . . . A'ight? I'll be right back."

Lil' Nicky slid into the driver's seat and waited.

About five minutes later, DeMarco came back and got into the truck.

"A'ight, Lil' Nicky, here's my number and five. Call me when you reach ya hood. Be safe, man, and dump this whip the first chance you get." DeMarco reached over to give him dap.

"I got you. Thanks, man, I appreciate it. You be safe too, a'ight?"

DeMarco watched as Lil' Nicky pulled off.

"Coolest white boy I know," he said aloud as he turned and walked away. "I'm back, bitches!" he yelled with a devilish grin.

CHAPTER FOUR

"Boy, stop standing around looking like you lost," De-Marco's Aunt V. said.

"Auntie, it just feels so good to be back home," De-Marco responded with a smile.

"Um huh, I still don't see why them people let you go early and didn't call to tell nobody."

"I told you, they took time off because I was bein good."

Aunt V. shook her head, knowing damn well he was lying; she'd let him think she was oblivious for the time being. "Boy, get in here so you can eat," she said, walking back into the house.

"A'ight," he replied before taking a quick look at his surroundings once more. Being on the run had him checking his back every other minute—he was betting that they wouldn't look for him at his aunt's place.

After he ate, DeMarco realized just how exhausted he was. He felt beat now that all the adrenaline had worn off. He went into one of the extra rooms and dropped back on the bed. As soon as he got comfortable, he fell right out, not even remembering to call Mrs. B like he told her he would.

"Damn, boy, you must've been tired; you slept all day and night," Aunt V. said the next morning.

"I did? Yesterday was a long day for me." DeMarco took a seat at the kitchen table as his aunt stood at the sink washing dishes.

"Nice to see you home, nigga," his cousin Money greeted, walking into the kitchen.

"Nigga, it's nice to be home," DeMarco said, smiling.

"Well, you know we got some catchin up to do. I'ma get up wit you though. I gotta make a couple of moves," Money said, and turned to leave.

"No doubt."

"So what you gonna be doin wit yourself?" Aunt V. asked.

"I'ma see if Uncle Br—"

"I don't think so. Me and Momma Paula got just the thing for you. As a matter of fact, wait here a minute," she said. She got up and left the kitchen, returning a few minutes later with a brown paper bag and some money. "Take it and drop this bag off around the way—that's your job from now on. I don't wanna see you standin on no damn block callin yourself a hustler! You hear me?"

"Yes, I got you, auntie," he said, getting up and leaving.

***

The weeks flew by for DeMarco. Between chilling with his cousin Money and running around, he was keeping himself busy.

One day while they were chilling, DeMarco noticed Money making a sale.

"Ayo, Money, you hustlin dope?" DeMarco asked, surprised.

"Nigga, this my own shit! Mommy and them pay me a'ight, but what they pay me for a week I see in a couple hours, or a day at the most."

DeMarco didn't know how much Aunt V. or Momma Paula were paying Money, but he was getting $800 a week. He figured Money was getting more than that and did some quick math in his head. Just as he was about to question Money some more, their cousin Steph walked up on them.

"Wassup, cuz?" Steph said, giving DeMarco a hug.

"Ain't shit, girl. Just chillin."

"Wassup, Money?"

"Shit, what's good wit you? When you gonna take some of this work and hold it down for me in the spot?" Money asked her.

"Boy, please! Auntie and them would kill us both," she said.

DeMarco sat listening to his cousins talk until he felt his pager vibrating. Looking at the number, he realized it was Momma Paula.

"Ayo, I gotta make a run. I'll get up wit y'all later," DeMarco said, and started walking off.

"Ayo, DeMarco, wait up. I'm goin that way," Steph said, running up beside him. "So wassup with you?"

"Ain't shit, just tryna stack some money, so I can snatch this whip."

"How much you need?" she asked.

"$1,100," he replied.

"What you got now?"

"Girl, I ain't tellin you how much bread I got." He stopped walking. Even though they were blood, he didn't trust anyone enough to say how much money he had.

"Boy, I don't want your money," she countered, punching him in the arm. "Just know if you need me for anything, holla at me." She gave him a quick hug before turning to walk away.

After making his drops for the day, DeMarco sat in his room and counted all the money he had saved up so far.

$3,500. Damn, I'm still $7,500 short. Fucking with auntie and them it will take me three, four more months to cop this whip, DeMarco thought to himself, and then put the rubber band back around his knot. Placing it back in the shoe box, he tried to figure out how he could make a quick come-up. He thought about Steph and what she'd said. Maybe she had a connection for him or maybe Money could put him on. His aunts would be pissed, but he needed to figure something out sooner than later.

The next morning, DeMarco was up early. He got dressed and headed downstairs, not surprised to see his aunts sitting in the kitchen.

"Wassup, aunties?" he asked, before giving them each a kiss on their cheek.

"Shit, you up early today. What you about to get into?" Momma Paula asked.

"I fell out early last night, so I'm well energized, plus I got a couple of things I need to handle," he said.

"A'ight, well, just be in the area around 1:00," Aunt V. said.

"I won't be far," he replied, and left without eating. He was focused on finding his cousin and seeing if she could really put him on.

He walked around the block to 118th where he figured Steph would be, but was pissed when he didn't see her. *Damn, where the fuck is this girl at?* he wondered.

His stomach started growling, so he walked to the closet corner store to grab something to snack on. He came out of the store a couple minutes later with a bag of chips and a Pepsi and started heading back up the block. He continued on his mission to find his cousin, but before he did a light-skinned chick with a fat ass distracted him. She was on the other side of the street, but he wasn't about to let her get out of his sight.

Damn, he thought as he yelled out, "Ayo, shorty, can I get a minute of your time?" Looking around as if there might be someone else with her, shorty stopped and stood looking at DeMarco as he came across the street. No doubt she was fine—he had to know her name. Standing there in a pair of Guess shorts that barely held her ass inside of them, and a Guess shirt with a pair of white 5411 Reebok Classics she had his full attention. He couldn't front: shorty was bad.

"Where you headed to, ma?" DeMarco asked.

"Why would I tell you that? I don't know you from a can of paint," she said.

"You don't have to act like that, yo. If I'm bothering you, I'll keep it moving."

"No, I'm sorry about that, it's just I'm annoyed as hell right now. I was supposed to meet my homegirl at the park, but she stood me up," shorty said.

"Come on. I'll chill with you in the park if you want some company. Do you mind?"

"Well, I don't got shit to do till later, so that's cool," she said, and they started walking toward the park.

DeMarco perched on the back of a bench and shorty sat down on the seat. "So what's your name?" he asked.

"Tiffany, but everybody calls me Tiff."

"I'm DeMarco. Nice to meet you Tiff," he said, causing her to smile. "So where you from?"

"I live in 40 projects with my sista when she's home," Tiff answered, pulling a piece of gum out of her pocket. "Want one?"

"Nah, I'm good, ma."

Sitting there talking to Tiff, he didn't realize how the time was passing until he felt his pager vibrate. *Damn*, he thought to himself as he clipped it back on his shorts.

"Tiff, I gotta go handle somethin, but I'm definitely tryna get up with you again," he said, getting down off the back of the bench.

"Okay, well, here go my number, just call me." Tiffany pulled a pen and piece of paper out of her pocket-book, then stood up. "I hope to hear from you," she said, licking her lips and walking off.

"Oh, no doubt you will," he replied, slipping the number in his pocket.

Back at the house, he went into the kitchen where he knew his aunt would be.

"Sorry about that, auntie, I kind of lost track of time," he said as he grabbed the bag off the table and turned to leave.

"Uh, some boy named Lil' Nicky called here for you," she told him.

"Word?" He stopped in his tracks.

"Yeah, he said he'd try you back later."

"Auntie, if I'm not here, can you give him my pager number?"

"I ain't your damn secretary! You need to go and get you a cell phone."

"I love you," he said, smiling, telling himself that once he made his drop he was going to do just that.

Coming from his last drop-off, he went to Queens Center mall, heading straight to the first cell phone store he saw.

He looked around for a minute or two before the store clerk approached.

"Can I help you?"

He turned around, but couldn't speak for a moment because the chick who stood in front of him had him completely mesmerized. She looked like a darker, younger version of Mrs. B.

"Can I help you?" she asked again.

"My fault, shorty, you just reminded me of some-body, but yeah, I need a phone," he replied.

"Okay, well, come this way." She led him to a display case. "Now, what kind of phone you looking for?"

"It don't even matter, yo, as long as it works." He was more interested in her than the phone.

"Okay, well, let me show you what we have."

Thirty minutes later, she was packing up his phone for him.

"Now, you can just throw the box out for me, if you don't mind, um . . ." he paused, realizing he hadn't got-ten her name.

"Jessica."

"Thanks, Jessica."

After taking a few steps, he stopped and turned back to her. "Ayo, Jess, you can use that number anytime," he said, and then walked out of the store.

Leaving Queens Center, DeMarco saw a gray Acura Legend and thought of the one he wanted. *Man, where my cousin at?*

Getting back to the block, DeMarco passed the crib and headed around the corner to 118th to see if he could run into Steph. He saw everyone else except her. He was almost about to give up, when she came walking around the corner.

"Wassup, cuz?" he said. "Yo, I been lookin for you all mornin."

"I stayed over at a friend's house uptown yesterday. But what up though?"

"Come on, let's hit the park and talk," he said.

Stopping at the same bench him and shorty had sat on earlier, DeMarco started laughing.

"Nigga, what's so funny?" Steph asked.

"Just thinkin about somethin. But yo, on some real shit, cuz, when you said I can ask you for help, what did you mean by that?"

"Just what I said. You my favorite cousin. When I was out here fucked up, you was the only one that didn't look at me different. Wassup? Talk to me."

Taking a deep breath, he said, "Listen, Steph. Fuckin with auntie and them is all good, but I see the money out here and I want in."

"So?"

"So I need ya help. You know I can't let auntie and them see me hustlin, and even if I did, they ain't gonna sell me shit anyway. I know you know people, plus you in the spot every day. You know all the heads that come through."

She sat quietly for a bit before jumping up suddenly and smiling. "Nigga, let's get it," she said. "What you got to spend?"

"Like $4,300," he replied.

"A'ight, meet me here at 6. I'll make a few calls."

"I'll be here. I love you cuz, on some real shit," he said, before giving her a quick hug.

They both left the park and went their separate ways.

Having a couple of hours to just chill until he had to

meet back up with Steph, DeMarco pulled out his phone and dialed a number that he could never forget. When no one answered, he hung up. Then he spotted his cousin Money sitting on the porch in front of his aunt's house.

"Wassup, Money?"

"Nothin, just waitin for this shorty to come holla at me," he replied.

"Nigga, when you gonna tell Tonya to hook me up with one of her girls?"

"Why you won't tell Tonya yourself?" Tonya said, approaching from behind.

"Girl, you better start making some noise when you walkin up on people," DeMarco said as Tonya stood there laughing. "I know you got some bad-ass friends. You can hook me up?"

"I'll see what I can do," she responded, climbing up the steps and into the house.

"Oh shit, look who it is," Money said, as a black-on-black BMW pulled up in front of them.

"Wassup?" DeMarco said as his Uncle Bruh got out of his whip.

"Same shit, nephew. Paula in the house?" Uncle Bruh asked, shaking his hand.

"Nah, I ain't see her all day," Money said. "Ayo, when you gonna let me drive?"

"Nigga, all the money I hear you around here trickin off, you coulda bought you some wheels," Uncle Bruh said, laughing as he got back into his car. "I'll catch you lil' niggas later."

"A'ight, unc," DeMarco said before walking inside.

He hung around the house until it was time to head back out to meet Steph. He arrived a few minutes late, but as promised, she was waiting for him.

"It's about time, nigga," she said as he sat down next to her. "Don't get comfortable, we gotta take a lil' ride."

They headed to the subway station and jumped on a train heading to an unknown destination.

"Ayo, cuz, where we goin?" he finally asked, once they sat down.

"Uptown, nigga, where else?" Steph replied with a crooked grin.

DeMarco stood next to Steph while she did business. Deciding to spend only $2,800, Steph talked homeboy into giving them 120 grams.

Forty-five minutes later, DeMarco sat in Steph's crib watching her bag up the product.

"You see, cuz, you chop it up into the size of rocks you want 'em to be, then put 'em in the capsule. Everybody over there selling dimes and better, but we gonna fuck the game up and sell nickels," Steph said, pushing the plate of rocks into the middle of the table.

An hour and a half later, DeMarco sat at the table with his cousin looking at all the capsules packed up and ready for distribution.

"That's $10,500," she said.

Damn! he thought to himself as he started calculating in his head. "A'ight, cuz, I trust you. You know we gotta keep this between us. Auntie and them can't find out about none of this," he said, getting ready to leave.

"I'll never do you wrong. I got you," Steph replied, looking into his eyes.

"A'ight, I'll get with you tomorrow."

Feeling good, DeMarco headed back around the way, thinking about how shit was about to go down. Digging into his pocket for his phone, he felt a piece of paper and pulled it out. He'd forgotten all about the shorty he'd met. He decided to give her a call.

"Hello," a female said on the third ring.

"Can I speak to Tiffany?"

"This is Tiffany. Who dis?"

"What's good, ma? Dis DeMarco."

"I ain't think you was gon call." He could hear the smile in her voice.

"I told you I would. So what you up to?" he asked.

"Nothin, just sittin here smokin."

"Now that's what I'm talkin 'bout."

"You said that like you was on your way here," she laughed.

"Soon as you give me the apartment number."

"306."

"A'ight. Got you. On my way!"

DeMarco flagged down a cab and told the driver where he wanted to go. He sat back thinking about what he was going to do to shorty. When they pulled up in front of the building, he paid the driver, then got out and headed up to her third-floor apartment. He knocked a few times with no answer. After a minute passed and nobody came to the door, he knocked again. Still no answer. He began to pull out his phone and was about to call her when he heard the chain slide from the other side. The door opened and Tiff was just standing there in a red bra and short-shorts, looking good enough to eat. He was speechless as he looked her up and down.

"You comin in?" she asked, smiling and stepping to the side. She led him to the living room where she had a movie playing.

"*Scarface*! This is my shit!" he said as he sat down on the sofa.

"This is one of my favorite movies." She picked up a Dutch from off the table and started cracking it open.

Two blunts later, they both sat high as a kite. De-Marco was relaxed and deep into the movie when he felt Tiffany going for the zipper on his pants. He looked over at her and didn't say a word as she pulled his dick through his boxers and wrapped her lips around it.

"Damn, girl," he finally said, looking down at her sucking his dick like a professional.

"You like that?" she asked, coming up for air.

"Definitely. Don't stop." He pushed her head back down on his dick.

Thirty minutes later she was still sucking, and it felt so good he had to stop her. "Easy, girl. Get up and take those clothes off."

Tiffany stood up and started coming out of the little bit of clothes she had on, bra first. When she pulled off her shorts and panties, her pretty pussy put him in a trance. It was perfectly trimmed and fat as hell.

"Come sit on this pole," he said, pulling off his clothes.

Straddling him, Tiffany grabbed his dick with her right hand and held it while she slid down on him. "Oh shit," she gasped.

With his dick inside of her, moving slowly at first, she worked him as her pussy grew wet. After a few minutes, she picked up speed, putting one of her feet on the sofa and riding him in a squatting position. She was bouncing up and down and the sound of her ass slapping against his thighs was driving him insane. He flipped her over on the couch and pulled her legs up on his shoulders. She moaned loudly as he slid all the way inside her. He spread her legs open wider by her ankles and started pounding on her pussy fast and deep.

"Oooh, yes. Just like that!" she yelled.

He continued fucking her for the next hour, until he nutted all over her stomach. He could get used to being with her. For a young girl, she knew how to make a nigga feel good. The pussy was so good it knocked him out. He slept like a baby with no intention of going home.

CHAPTER FIVE

DeMarco woke up the next morning in a daze. He looked over at Tiffany, who was asleep next to him. He eased out of the bed, trying not to wake her. He walked into the bathroom pulling out his semihard dick on the way to the toilet and noticed for the first time someone standing there butt-ass naked looking at him.

"Oh shit, my fault," he said, still holding his dick in his hand.

"That's a'ight, go ahead and use the bathroom," she said, staring down at his hand. "I'm Sharon, Tiff's older sister."

He wasn't uncomfortable with her presence. He was working with the right tools; even semihard, it was larger than most. After flushing the toilet he walked over to the sink to wash his hands. He glanced over at Sharon's nakedness. She hadn't even attempted to conceal her birthday suit. His eyes moved from top to bottom and stopped at her shaved pussy. His dick was now hard as a brick.

"And your name is . . . ?" she asked, pulling him out of his trance as she slid on a thong.

"DeMarco."

"Well, nice to meet you, DeMarco. Now I gotta finished gettin dressed before I'm late for work." Sharon pulled on a matching bra over her firm titties.

"Yeah, nice to meet you too," he said.

She laughed as he walked out.

DeMarco put on his clothes as he looked at Tiffany sleeping. Finding a pen and paper, he wrote a quick note with his number on it before leaving the room. Sharon was standing in the doorway putting lotion on her body. She looked up and smiled before she pushed the door closed. Laughing to himself, he headed to the front door and let himself out.

Back at the crib, DeMarco walked straight upstairs to take a shower. After getting dressed, he went into the kitchen where his aunts were sitting talking to his cousin. Money had his head down on the table and was being scolded.

"See, I bet you learned your lesson now," Momma Paula said as Aunt V. just chuckled.

"What I miss?" DeMarco asked, sitting down at the table.

"Fuckin wit them dumb-ass bitches out there last night, ya dumb-ass cousin got jumped by some dude," Momma Paula replied.

"What?!" DeMarco yelled, leaping up from his chair. "Nah, niggas ain't gonna jump my family. Money, where them niggas at?"

"Boy, sit down! Ain't nobody jump nobody. They fought right there out front. He let some lil' 5'3" shrimp whip his ass," Aunt V. said before laughing again.

Looking at Money with his head still on the table and not saying anything, DeMarco sat back down and burst out laughing too.

"Money, tell me they lyin, yo. Tell me you ain't let some lil' nigga whip you out," DeMarco said.

"Man, shut the fuck up, DeMarco!" Money yelled.

"Wow, gangster, don't get mad at me! I ain't the one that whipped you out."

"A'ight, that's enough. Boy, don't you have somethin to do?" Momma Paula said to DeMarco.

"Yeah, I'm gone." DeMarco grabbed the bag off the table and shook his head as he left the kitchen. He could hear Aunt V. giggling as he headed out of the house.

After finishing his drops, DeMarco returned home. He was sitting on the porch shooting the breeze with Money when his aunt came to the door to give him the phone. It was Lil' Nicky.

"Lil' Nicky, wassup wit you, nigga? When my aunt told me you called and then didn't call back again, I thought they caught you."

"Man, fuck them niggas," Lil' Nicky replied. "They ain't gettin me again. But yo, I need to holla at you in a minute."

"When you ready just holla, a'ight? Take my cell number," DeMarco said.

"A'ight, let me go finish makin these moves. I'ma holla at you soon."

"A'ight, Lil' Nicky, make sure you holla at me. You know I got you," he said before they hung up.

"Wassup, cuz. You smokin yet?" Money asked as he lit the blunt he'd just finished rolling.

"Nigga, why wouldn't I be?" DeMarco replied as his cell phone rang. "Yo, who dis?"

"Um, can I speak to DeMarco?" a female voice asked.

"This him. Who dis?"

"This is Jessica from the cell phone store."

"Oh, wassup, sexy?"

"Nothing. I just decided to call to see what was up with you. You did say I could use the number," she said.

"That I did. I ain't doin too much. Just sittin here chillin with my cousin. Why, what's good?"

"I was just wondering if you wanted to chill tonight. Go see a movie or somethin."

"If it's with you, I'm down," he replied with a chuckle.

"Well, okay, um, I live in Harlem, but I can meet you or come pick you up if you want."

"You know where 119th and Merrick Boulevard is?"

"Yeah, I know where that's at."

"Okay, then I'm right there at my auntie's house," he said.

"Cool, just stay right there. I'll be there in a minute."

"Got you," he replied and hung up.

"Nigga, who was that?" Money asked as he passed DeMarco the blunt.

"This dark-skinned chick from the cell phone store over at Queens Center," he said.

"The one that look like she could be Stacey Dash's daughter?" Money asked.

"Yeah, that's the one," DeMarco replied with a big smile.

"Fuck outta here, nigga! Shorty like twenty-five-plus. Everybody that go in there be tryna holla at shorty, and she shoot niggas down daily," Money said with a twisted lip.

"You'll see when she get here, and remember I ain't everybody," DeMarco said with a laugh.

"Yeah, we'll see."

Still laughing, DeMarco passed the blunt back to Money as his phone began to ring again. "Yo," he said.

"Hey, DeMarco, it's Tiff. Wassup, wit you?"

"Shit, wassup wit you?"

"I was just sittin here wonderin if you were comin through tonight."

"Nah, I can't. I got some shit I gotta take care of, but I'ma holla at you if plans change. A'ight?"

"A'ight, hopefully I'll see you soon. Oh, before I go, my sister said wassup, and next time don't look so shocked. Whatever that's supposed to mean."

"Nah, tell her I said wassup and I wasn't shocked, she just caught me by surprise, that's all," he said with a grin.

"A'ight, then, call me later," Tiffany replied.

"I got you," he said before hanging up and putting

his phone down next to him. He picked up a Dutch and started cracking it down the middle. "Ayo, Money, what time is it?"

"Ten after seven," Money replied, looking down at his phone.

Taking the blunt from Money, DeMarco was growing impatient. He was about to say fuck it and call Tiff back, when a black Honda Accord pulled up in front of the house.

"Who that?" Money asked, trying to see through the tinted windows.

"I don't know." DeMarco stood up to get a better view.

The driver's-side door opened and Money's jaw dropped. "Hell no!" he shouted as Jessica stepped out of the car.

DeMarco walked down the steps to meet her. He reached out and gave her a hug. "You're lookin good," he said, enjoying the view. She was dressed in a pair of tight jeans and a tank top that showed all of her curves. He was damn near drooling thinking about tapping that.

"You're lookin good yourself," she said, smiling.

Money cleared his throat.

"Oh, my fault. Jessica, I want you to meet my cousin Money."

"How you doin, Money? I've seen you a couple times in the store, right?"

"Yeah, you did," Money replied, excited that she remembered.

"A'ight then, cuz, I'll holla at you later," DeMarco

said as he and Jessica walked back to her whip. Getting in, he looked over at Money and laughed as they pulled off.

As she maneuvered through traffic, DeMarco couldn't help but stare. She looked much different than the average around-the-way girl. She was sexy, but not trashy.

"If you live all the way in Harlem, what you doin workin in Queens?" DeMarco asked.

"Well, my cousin used to work there," she replied. "When I came up here from Georgia, I moved in with her and she got me the job."

"So where are we headed?" DeMarco asked.

"I thought we could go uptown to Willie's Burgers for somethin to eat," she replied.

"That's cool with me. I'm your prisoner until you drop me back off," he said, making her laugh.

"You're crazy."

"Yeah, I've been told that a lot, but at least it's crazy in a good way," DeMarco said, still laughing.

After eating, they rode around the city for a while. Neither of them was ready to call it a night, so they sat parked outside his house and talked. Even though he wanted to bend her over, there was something about her that made him want to get to know her on a deeper level.

"So when we gonna do this again?" she asked.

"You call, I'll come," he said.

"You're too much," she chuckled.

"I know, but for real, whenever you get time, you got

my number, and next time it's on me," DeMarco said.

"That's a deal," she smiled.

"A'ight, so let me let you go, so you won't be all tired at work tomorrow," he said, leaning over and giving her a hug.

"See you soon, crazy," she said as he got out.

"Looking forward to it," he replied.

As she pulled off, DeMarco looked at his phone and saw that he had seven missed calls. He checked the time of the last one—12:30 a.m.—and decided not to call back since it was already 1:15. Entering the house, he said hello to his Aunt V. and went to his room. Closing the door behind him, he kicked off his sneakers, jeans, and fell back onto the bed. Just as he was about to fall asleep, his pager went off, but he decided to ignore it.

His pager was blowing up again. He snatched it off the nightstand and looked at it. *Damn, who the fuck is this?* he thought, remembering the same number from the night before.

"Hello," a female voice said after the third ring.

"Who dis? Somebody paged me from here?" De-Marco asked.

"Yeah, nigga, it's your fucking cousin!" Steph yelled.

"Oh, wassup, cuz?"

"Don't *wassup* me, nigga, where the hell you at?" she asked.

"At the house, why?"

"I need to see you *now*. We got a problem."

"Where you at?" DeMarco asked.

"Just meet me at my house," she said, and hung up.

DeMarco hurried up and got dressed, trying to figure out what the problem could be. All sorts of things were going through his mind. Twenty minutes later he was banging on her door.

"Boy, why you hammerin on my door like you the damn police?" she said as she let him in.

"You said we had a problem, so I'm anxious. What happened?" He followed her into the living room where she had money stacked up on the table.

"Nigga, this is what happened, and it would have been more if your punk ass would have answered my pages last night," she said, pointing to the table. "$10,450!"

"In two days?" DeMarco asked with amazement.

"More like a day and a half," she replied.

"Damn, cuz," he said while shaking his head.

"Ummm, no shit. Why the fuck you think I've been pagin yo ass all night like that? We gotta re-up!" Steph said in a serious tone.

"Well let's go, 'cause we droppin $5,000 this time," he said as they headed out the door.

CHAPTER SIX

After a month of fucking with his cousin, DeMarco was sitting on close to $25,000, not even counting the $11,000 he had in his pocket. He was on his way to get a car and it was long overdue. Walking into the car lot, he spotted a black Nissan Maxima. Jimmy, the salesman, was speaking to a coworker when he noticed DeMarco looking around.

"If you like that, I've got something you'll love," Jimmy said, strolling over to a silver Acura Legend sitting on chrome BBS rims.

"Yeah, this is it! I got $11,000 cash down," DeMarco said, digging in his pocket and pulling out his wad of cash.

"That'll work, let's go over to my office," Jimmy replied, as they both walked together.

After the two discussed the terms, Jimmy passed him the keys. DeMarco pulled out of the dealership ready to roll through the hood in his new whip. His mind quickly jumped to his plans for that night and how he was sup-posed to meet Money at the skating rink. From what his cousin said, Tonya had a friend who made Jessica look like second best.

He had a little time to waste, so he called Tiffany up. He'd missed her call while he was handling business.

"Wassup, Tiff? You called me?"

"Yes, I was wondering if you were gonna come by," she asked.

"You know what, Tiff? Once I get dressed, I'll slide through for a little while, a'ight?"

"A'ight, I'll be waiting," she said as she hung up.

Twenty minutes later, he stepped out of the shower and got dressed, slipping on a pair of Tommy Hilfiger sweats and matching t-shirt. He grabbed a cab and made his way over to her apartment. The door was unlocked, so he let himself in. Tiff was sitting in her room watch-ing TV.

"I missed you," she said.

"Oh yeah, how much?" he asked with a slight smile.

"A lot," she replied in a seductive tone.

"Show me how much," he said as he pulled his dick out.

She didn't waste any time giving him head. He leaned back on his elbows as Tiffany crawled between his legs on the floor. He closed his eyes for a few sec-onds and listened to the slurping noises. But feeling like somebody was watching him, he opened his eyes. To his surprise, Sharon was standing there by the door watch-ing. She moved into the room slowly while putting one of her hands down her pants. He could see her rubbing on her pussy.

You like? he mouthed.

Sharon nodded her head yes.

He waved her over with his free hand.

"Let me help you with that, lil' sis," Sharon said, staring at her sister for a minute.

Looking up, Tiffany pulled DeMarco's pants all the way down. As Sharon wrapped her lips around his dick, Tiffany played with his balls. Sharon took him deeper and deeper into her throat. After fifteen minutes of this tag-team routine, he told them both to get out of their clothes. Sitting back on the bed looking at the sisters standing in front of him naked, he'd forgotten all about meeting up with Money.

"Sharon, I want you to climb on up on this dick, and Tiff, you bring that pretty-ass pussy over here so I can taste it," he instructed. "Tonight is about to get crazy."

As Sharon slid down, her pussy gripped his dick like it was custom-made for him. Tiffany climbed up top and rode his face, rubbing pussy juice all over his lips.

"Oh my god! This is why my sister is so open?! Damn, this dick is good," Sharon mumbled as she bounced up and down with her firm titties bobbing all over the place.

At eighteen, DeMarco was doing shit that niggas twice his age only dreamed about. "Yeah, bounce on this dick!"

At this moment it was confirmed that he was the man. Then, after fucking both sisters, he dozed off on the sofa.

***

He thought he was dreaming when he felt someone straddle his lap. He opened his eyes to find Sharon rubbing his dick on her wet pussy.

"Just lay back and let me do this. I didn't want to show my sister up last night too much, but she went somewhere, so let me really get right," Sharon said, putting her hands on his chest. She leaned forward and began moving back and forth, slowly at first. His dick got harder as she started to rock faster. Rising to her feet, she started bouncing on his dick like she was on a pogo stick.

"Damn, girl," he said, gritting his teeth.

"Yessss, yes, yes, that's what the fuck I'm talkin about!" she yelled.

"Move to the end of the couch," he said.

Sharon slid in between his legs with her back toward him as he slipped back inside of her. She bent over with her hands on the floor, slamming her ass up and down like she was in a porno movie.

"Damn, this pussy is so good," he moaned, slapping her butt.

"Yes, spank that ass!" she shouted, looking up over her shoulder at him. "You ready for this?" she asked.

"Bring it. I'm ready for whatever you throw my way," he said as he bit his bottom lip; her pussy was as wet as a faucet.

She pulled his dick out and slid it in her ass in one smooth motion, shocking the shit out of him.

"Yessss," she cried out as her ass swallowed his entire length.

"Oh my god!" she screamed. Lost in the moment, he started bouncing her up and down on his dick with his hands around her waist.

When she felt him tense up, Sharon bounced on him a couple more times before getting up off him. Kneeling down between his legs, she took his dick in her mouth and started sucking it like she learned from the porn bitch Vanessa del Rio or something. It felt so good that DeMarco closed his eyes and gritted his teeth. He couldn't hold back any longer as she did her thing. He sat up and opened his eyes to find Sharon staring at him. Just the look on her face sent him overboard. Grabbing a handful of her hair, he pulled her head back as he stood up and started cumming. All the while Sharon had his dick secure in her mouth like she had lockjaw or something. He peered down at her as he nutted and she tried to keep it all in her mouth. Cum spilled out of the sides of her lips, dripping down her chin.

He fell back on the sofa exhausted. She followed him with his dick still in her mouth, sucking him until there wasn't a drop left. Satisfied, she stood up and smiled down at him.

"Now that's some shit to wake up to," he said as she licked her fingers.

"Anytime," she replied, then turned and left the room.

"Damn," was all he could say as he watched her walk away, shaking her ass. Hearing his phone ring, he bent over and pulled it out of his sweats.

"Yo, who dis?" he asked.

"Nigga, who you think it is? How you gonna stand

me up like that last night? Tonya talking mad shit!" Money yelled.

"Ayo, cuz, my fault. I got caught up in some crazy shit last night. Word! I'm telling you, this shit was crazy. But where you at?" DeMarco asked.

"I'm at the house," Money replied.

"A'ight, I'll be there in like a half hour," DeMarco said with a rushed tone.

He quickly put on his clothes, making sure he didn't forget anything. On his way out, he ran into Sharon.

"Ayo, tell Tiff I'ma get up with her later."

"You know I got you," Sharon said, grabbing his dick and sucking on his ear.

"Damn, what you tryna do, get me open?"

"Nigga, ya lil' ass already got me open, right along with my sista," she said, smiling.

Shaking his head, he walked out the door.

"Well, if it ain't Mr. Stand Niggas Up," Money said, as DeMarco walked up to the porch.

"Don't start the bullshit! I said it was my fault. I got caught up in some shit," DeMarco replied. "So wassup with you, cuz?" he said.

"Shit's been crazy for me. I caught one of my friends comin out the spot on 119th," Money said. "Ayo, I'm tellin you, whoever got up in that joint got shit poppin off the hook over there. I asked Steph, but she said she didn't know who them niggas was."

"Fuck 'em! We already eatin wit auntie and them," DeMarco said with a grin.

Money had no idea that DeMarco was the one supplying the spot.

"Ayo, so wassup wit shorty, yo?" DeMarco asked, changing the subject. He wasn't ready for Money to find out about his side hustle.

"Who?" Money asked.

"Tonya's friend, nigga!" DeMarco said.

"Oh, LaLa? I don't know. Shorty be with Tonya sometimes. I know she was talkin shit when you ain't show up, like, *That's why I don't fuck with niggas now.* She left the rink early," Money said.

Once again, DeMarco's cell phone rang.

"Yo, who dis?" he said.

"It's Jessica, baby."

"Oh, wassup, ma?" he replied with a smile on his face.

"Are you busy right now?" she asked.

"Nah, why?" he replied.

"Well, I'ma come get you. I need to talk to you," she said.

"A'ight, I'm at the crib," DeMarco replied.

"Okay, I'll be there in like ten or fifteen minutes," she said in a serious voice.

"A'ight," he said. He wasn't sure what she wanted to talk about, but he was definitely anxious to know.

When she pulled up twenty minutes later, DeMarco stood and walked down the steps. "Money, I'll get up with you later, cuz," he said before stepping into the car.

As Jessica pulled off, he looked at her and felt his

dick start to get hard. Just thinking about how badly he wanted to fuck her drove him wild.

"Wassup, ma?" he asked after a few minutes.

"I need you to do me two favors. I'm about to go back home for a couple days and when I get back, I'ma need your help with somethin, but I'll explain what it is in a little bit," she said, hoping DeMarco would agree to help her.

"Okay, when you leaving?" he asked.

"Tonight," she replied.

"A'ight, and the second favor?" he asked, with a puzzled look on his face.

"I need some of this," she said, reaching her right hand over and rubbing his dick.

"You know you don't even have to ask twice," he said, as he realized Jessica was pulling into a hotel parking lot. All he could do was smile when she pulled up to the spot. Ten minutes later he was lying back on the bed while Jessica had her juicy lips wrapped around his dick.

A few hours later, as Jessica was taking him back to his crib, his phone rang.

"Yo, who dis?" he asked.

"Um, can I speak to Mr. Jones?" a male voice replied.

"This him," DeMarco said.

"Just wanted to let you know that your car is ready to be picked up," the guy said.

"A'ight, bet, I'm on my way," DeMarco said and hung up. "Can you do me a favor and drop me off at my car?" he asked Jessica.

"Sure, that's the least I can do after what you did for me," she replied with a smile.

They pulled up to the shop to find his car sitting outside.

"Damn, that Legend looks official," she said.

"Yeah, that shit tight, ain't it?"

DeMarco went inside to handle the business with the manager and returned a few minutes later.

"What time does your bus leave?" he asked Jessica.

"At 7:00," she replied.

"It's 6:35 now, so go ahead so you don't miss your bus," he said.

"Okay. You make sure I get a ride in that when I get back," Jessica said, with a smile.

"I'll give you more than a ride." He bent over to give her a kiss and said goodbye, then watched her drive away. He walked over to the car and used the keypad to unlock the doors. He started his whip and pulled off.

Watch niggas hate! he thought to himself as he turned on the radio. Hearing his sound system come to life, he grinned wide. "Now that's what the fuck I'm talkin about!" he shouted.

Driving around, he didn't realize how late it was until he pulled into a McDonald's parking lot and his phone began to ring.

"Yeah, who dis?" he asked.

"Ayo, cuz, it's your lucky day. You got another chance to meet shorty. Her and Tonya on they way over here. Tonya wanna go see a movie. You wit it?" Money asked.

"Yeah, I'm wit it. I'll be there in like fifteen minutes."

DeMarco threw the phone on the passenger seat and pulled out of the parking lot. He had his windows down and was bumping Biggie's joint "Juicy" when he pulled up in front of his aunt's house. He sat there looking at his cousin checking out the car and laughed. He was about to call him, but then stopped, seeing Tonya come out of the house, followed by the baddest brown-skinned chick he'd ever seen in the hood. She was standing there in a pair of open-toed heels and a wraparound skirt that came down a little past her knees with a shirt to match; the outfit showed off her figure. She was blessed with a body that looked like she should be in a fashion magazine or rap video.

Turning the music down, DeMarco opened his door and got out.

"Get the fuck outta here!" Money said.

Laughing, DeMarco walked up to Tonya's friend. "How you doin, Ms. LaLa?"

"Just LaLa, no Ms.," she said, looking him up and down. "You must be Mr. Stand People Up?"

"My fault about that. I got caught up in something, but I'm DeMarco."

"Well, nice to meet you, DeMarco," she replied.

"Definitely nice to finally meet you," he said with a little grin on his face.

"Okay, now that all that's out the way, cuz, when you cop the whip? That shit fire!" Money said, walking over to the car.

"Like two days ago, but I left it at the shop, so the music and shit could be put in it."

"Man, you know you gonna let me whip that, right?" his cousin said, grinning from ear to ear.

"Yeah, I hear you," DeMarco said.

"Um, if you two are done now, can we go?" Tonya asked, then she and LaLa started laughing.

"Yeah, let's go," DeMarco said.

They all piled into his car and set off for the movie. DeMarco and LaLa immediately hit it off. He was looking forward to getting to know her better. He was also looking forward to tapping that fat ass of hers.

For the next week, DeMarco and LaLa talked on the phone three or four times a day. She even called him in the middle of one of his episodes with Tiffany and Sharon.

Business was going well, with Lil' Nicky coming down buying five ounces from him every two weeks. He had his own spot now, but still kept his money at his aunt's crib.

Sitting back just chilling one afternoon after bagging up with Steph, he realized that it had been nearly a week since Jessica had left and he hadn't heard from her. He'd even called her a few times, to no avail. Having some time on his hands, he went over to his aunt's house to talk to Money. Walking into Money's room without knocking, he found his cousin counting a stack of cash.

"Nigga, you don't know how to knock?" Money threw the covers from his bed over his cash.

"Nigga, I don't care about ya bread," DeMarco said, sitting down at the foot of the bed. Grabbing the remote, he started flipping through the channels, stopping on the 5 o'clock news.

"Now for the top story. I stand in front of the Port Authority where sometime last night a female was arrested by the NYPD and was found in possession of two and a half kilos of cocaine. Twenty-four-year-old Jessica Smith was followed from Georgia two days ago while on her way to New York City. No other known parties were arrested with her."

"Get the fuck outta here!" Money said, taking the words right out of DeMarco's mouth. They sat there staring at Jessica's picture on the TV.

"From what we've been told," the reporter continued, *"it seems she is part of an all-female ring that smuggles drugs from Georgia to New York City, Boston, Connecticut, and Philadelphia. A tip was given that Ms. Smith was on her way back to New York by way of bus, in possession of a large amount of cocaine."*

Hitting the *off* button, DeMarco sat back, not wanting to hear any more. "Damn!" he said, shaking his head.

CHAPTER SEVEN

By the age of nineteen, DeMarco had it made. He had his own crib, car, $40,000 in his stash, and one of the baddest bitches in the hood at arm's reach. He was shining so much that he had all kinds of older dudes trying to get him on their team. Fucking with a lot of dudes wasn't his thing. He didn't need to, since all he had to do was sit back and let his cousin move his work.

Pulling up in front of his aunt's crib one afternoon, he noticed his Uncle Bruh sitting on the porch. As soon as DeMarco got out of his car, his uncle stood up from his seat.

"Come on, nephew, take a ride wit me." Uncle Bruh walked over to his BMW. Getting in with him, DeMarco had a feeling there was something on his uncle's mind.

"So wassup, unc?" DeMarco asked.

"I've been watching you since you been home. Even when you think I don't see you, I do. And even though your aunts might not have caught on, I did. I know that you got Steph over there on 119th hustlin for you—"

"Nah, that ain't me, unc."

"Well, the point is, I want you to come fuck with me," Uncle Bruh said.

"Me? Why not Money?" DeMarco asked.

"'Cause Money was out here the whole time you was gone. You came home and still doin better than him."

Just as DeMarco was about to reply, Uncle Bruh pulled over and jumped out of the car.

"Ayo, Smoke! What? You thought you could duck me forever like the coward you are?" Uncle Bruh yelled, walking up on some light-skinned dude.

"Nah, it ain't even like that, Bruh," the guy replied, "I'm not—"

That was all the guy was able to get out before Uncle Bruh dropped him with a quick two-piece, and then started stomping him out. DeMarco heard bones break from where he sat in the car. Kicking him one last time in the face, Uncle Bruh spit on him and then walked back to the car, got in, and drove off like nothing ever happened.

"Like I was saying, nephew, I want you to be a part of my team. You'll only answer to me, and everything you're doin now, that's your business. Just think about it."

"A'ight, unc, I hear you. I'll think about it," DeMarco said as he got out, now back at his aunt's house.

He already knew he was going to say yes, but he didn't want his uncle to know he'd made up his mind. As Uncle Bruh drove off, DeMarco's cell phone began to ring.

"Yo," he said.

"Wassup, you?" the person replied.

"You wit your fine ass," he said.

"I like the sound of that," LaLa said.

"Oh yeah? Well, I can show you much more if you like that?" DeMarco replied.

"You never know. I just might. Where you at?" she asked.

"My aunt's crib," he said with quickness.

"You wanna go somewhere?" she asked, in a soft voice.

"Where?" he asked.

"Never mind where, do you wanna go or not?" LaLa replied with sass.

"Fuck it, why not. When?" DeMarco said, anxious to see her.

"Stay at your aunt's house and I'll be over there in ten minutes," she replied.

DeMarco sat inside of his car and rolled a blunt. He took a few puffs before LaLa came down the block. He put out his blunt in the ashtray and stepped from the car just as she reached him. He gave her a hug, inhaling the scent of her perfume.

"Wassup with you, sexy?" he said, looking her up and down.

"Just happy to see you. You ready?" she replied, while smiling and staring into his eyes.

"I was born ready, ma," he said as he started to walk around the car.

"Nah, I'll drive, this is a surprise," she said and then winked at him.

"Well then, it's all yours," he replied.

"Nah, it ain't yet, but it will be soon," she said, walking around to the driver's seat.

DeMarco climbed into the passenger's-side door and let his seat back as she started the car. It wasn't long before she was pulling into a Holiday Inn parking lot. He looked over at her and smiled. He knew exactly what time it was and he was down for it. When she got out of the car she turned back to him, and noticed he hadn't budged.

"You comin or not?" she asked.

Once they checked in and entered the room, he immediately took a seat on the bed.

"G'head, kick your shoes off. This is home for the night. I'ma go take a shower," she said, as she headed to the bathroom.

He removed his sneakers and grabbed the remote to turn on the TV. Flipping through the channels, he stopped on the old war movie *Hamburger Hill*, even though it was almost over. Remembering he had some bud in the whip, he went outside to get it. When he came back inside, he heard the shower still running. He sat back on the bed and cracked a Dutch down the middle. Emptying the guts into the trash can on the side of the bed, he rolled up and lit the blunt. Halfway through the smoke—and as the movie was ending—he looked over as the bathroom door opened. LaLa came out in a pair of boy shorts and a wifebeater with her hair in a ponytail. He could see that her nipples were semihard as she slid onto the bed next to him.

"What's coming on?" she asked.

"I don't know, it didn't say yet," he replied.

"Well, let's see what's on," she said, grabbing the remote. She flipped through the channels before settling on the Spike Lee classic *Do the Right Thing*. Putting the remote control down, she lifted his arm, so she could slide up under it.

Pulling her closer to him, he relaxed even more as he smoked the rest of his blunt. While watching the movie, he caught her staring at him from the corner of his eye. "What?" he asked.

"Nothing," she said, looking back at the TV.

Moving his arm down around her waist, he rolled her over, so that she was straddling his lap. "Wassup? Talk to me," he said, in a comforting voice.

"I can't fight it anymore," she said nervously.

"So don't fight it, just let shit take its course," he replied, as he gently held her hands.

"You're right," she said, as she bent over and kissed him.

Letting her hair down, she ran her hands under his shirt, rubbing him on his chest. Sitting up some, DeMarco removed his shirt as LaLa pulled the wifebeater over her head. He took one of her breasts into his mouth and started sucking it while playing with the other one. She moaned as he sent tingles all through her body.

"Get undressed," he said, as he rolled her over.

He stood up and took off the rest of his clothes and laid back down on the bed with her beside him. He pulled her closer as he kissed her. Rubbing her smooth skin and making his way down to her pussy, he started massaging her clit. He stuck two fingers inside of her wet pussy as she cried out and nibbled on his ear.

"It's been awhile, please be gentle," she whispered.

"I got you, ma," DeMarco said as he opened her legs wider. Taking hold of his dick, he gently rubbed it up and down her dripping wet pussy, teasing her with pleasure.

She reached down and grabbed his dick. "I need to feel you inside of me," she whispered.

DeMarco couldn't believe how tight and wet her pussy was. He fucked her slowly in every position he could. It wasn't long before she was screaming his name and digging her nails into his back.

"Oh my god! Oh my god! Ohhh my god, boy, you about to make me cum! I'm cumming, babbyyy!" She started shaking and locked her legs tightly around De-Marco's waist.

"La, I'm about to cum, let me pull out."

"No, go ahead, please," she said as she tightened her legs around him.

He started stroking her deeper and longer. DeMarco was about to bust when LaLa screamed out, "I'm cumming again!"

He nutted inside of her and immediately relaxed on top of her.

Hours later, as they laid in bed, DeMarco said, "La, I'm not gonna lie to you. As much as I would love to stay here longer, I can't. I need to get back to the hood."

"I know, I do too. I was just enjoying my time with you," she replied with a smile.

"A'ight, let me go clean up," he replied.

"Not before I take a ride," LaLa said as she got on top of DeMarco, taking his growing dick in her hand. She held it as she slid down on it, taking it all the way in. She let out a moan and started riding him like a trained horse jockey.

DeMarco pulled into LaLa's projects at 1:30 in the morning. Although it was late, there were still people hanging outside. He gave her a kiss as she got out.

"I'll call you once I've recuperated," she said with a smile.

"A'ight, ma," he said with a that's-my-pussy-now look on his face.

As she entered her building, DeMarco pulled off and headed back to his crib.

CHAPTER EIGHT

Damn, *it's almost 1!* DeMarco had slept through the morning and was already behind on his day. After getting dressed, DeMarco grabbed his cell, beeper, keys, and left the house. His first stop was to get his uncle's number from his aunt and then go talk to his cousin. He pulled up to his aunt's house a little while later and went inside.

"Wassup, aunties?"

"Where you been at, boy?" Aunt V. asked.

"I been around, was layin back with this chick I met," DeMarco said.

"Um, I bet you were doin more than just layin back," Momma Paula said with a chuckle.

"Ayo, Aunt V., you got Uncle Bruh's number?"

"What you want his number for?" Momma Paula asked.

"I just need to holla at him about a chick I mess wit—her aunt want to holla at him," he lied.

"Yeah, a'ight," his aunt said, giving him the number.

DeMarco sat and chatted with his aunts for a little while before he got up to leave. He was on his way over to see what was going on with Steph and the work. When he arrived at her house, she was outside sitting on the porch. Coming down the steps, she couldn't believe how ill his whip looked.

"Now you really shittin," she said, smiling.

"You did this for me, cuz," DeMarco replied.

She was surprised by the seriousness in his eyes. "It ain't about shit, cuz, you family. Now come on let me show you somethin," she said, as she turned and walked toward the crib. DeMarco followed her into the living room where there was money stacked on the table in six piles with rubber bands. "That's $30,000 right there, cuz! That's what I made while you was gone."

"Damn, cuz, you killing shit over here! I gotta go meet up with Uncle Bruh about somethin, but I'm gonna get back wit you later on," he said, picking up all the money and throwing it in a backpack.

"A'ight, get wit me because we have to re-up," she said.

"A'ight," he replied before heading out and getting in his car. He drove back over to the block and found his uncle's BMW sitting in front of the house.

When DeMarco started walking toward the car, the passenger's window rolled down.

"Wassup, nigga?" Chase said.

"Oh shit! What's good, Chase?" DeMarco said as he got in. "Nigga, I ain't seen you in a minute." He gave Chase a pound.

"Yo, a nigga been layin low, but ya uncle told me to come scoop you up," Chase said as he pulled off.

"Yeah, I see you shinin." DeMarco stared at his jewels.

"Fuckin wit ya uncle, nigga got my shit up, bitches be all over ya boy," Chase said.

"I hear that," DeMarco replied.

Thirty minutes later, Chase pulled into a long driveway. This was DeMarco's first visit to his Uncle Bruh's house. They parked and headed to the back where his uncle was sitting at the pool.

"What's good, nephew?" Uncle Bruh said, as he gave DeMarco a pound.

"Ain't shit, just chilling, you know me," he replied.

"Yeah, I feel that, nephew. So this is the role you'll be playing." He proceeded to break shit down for De-Marco. "So that's it, nephew. If there's a problem, I'll call you or Chase."

"Bet, unc," DeMarco said, distracted by a chick coming through the patio door.

"Bruh, the phone," she said as she walked over to him and handed him a phone.

"Who is it?" he asked her.

"That stupid girl of yours," she responded.

"Not now," he said into the phone, and then hung up. "Meesha, this is my nephew DeMarco, DeMarco this baby doll is Meesha."

"Nice to meet you, DeMarco."

"You too," he replied.

In his mind he was going crazy about how bad she

was. She was about 5'4" or 5'5", with a perfect Coca-Cola frame. She had a unique look you only see in magazines. When she turned to walk away in her two-piece bathing suit, he got a good look at all that ass and couldn't stop his dick from getting hard.

"Damn, unc, you like that?" DeMarco said.

"Yeah, that's me, lil' nigga, but you can get her little sister—she around here somewhere. Chase tried, but she shot him down," Uncle Bruh said, laughing.

"You still talkin about that shit, I see," Chase mumbled.

"Speaking of the devil," Chase said as Mia came out of the house.

"Wassup, big guy?" Mia greeted, hugging Uncle Bruh from behind.

"Same shit, where you been?" he asked.

"Out with some friends, but who is this?" She walked around Uncle Bruh to stand in front of DeMarco.

"DeMarco, this is Mia. Mia, this is my nephew DeMarco."

"What's good, Mia?" DeMarco said, checking her out. She looked just like her sister. Both were bad as fuck.

"Hopefully you," Mia said before she walked off.

"Ain't that a bitch," Chase said as DeMarco and Uncle Bruh busted out laughing.

It was 1 in the morning when DeMarco left Uncle Bruh's house. Not wanting Chase to know where he laid his head, DeMarco had him drop him back off at his aunt's crib. He needed to pick up his car anyway.

"A'ight, DeMarco, I'll get up with you in the a.m.," Chase said.

"No doubt, Chase, I'ma holla at you," DeMarco replied, stepping out of the car. He walked into the house to find LaLa wrapped up in a conversation with his two aunts.

"Wassup, you?" LaLa said.

"Nothin much, what are you doin here?" DeMarco asked.

"I told you we needed to talk," LaLa said as she got up off the couch. "We can do that when you droppin me home."

"A'ight, let's go. I'll see y'all later," DeMarco called out to his aunts as they left the house.

"So, wassup?" he asked as soon as they got into the car.

"This is for you." She pulled a paper bag out of her backpack when DeMarco stopped at a red light.

"What's dis?" he said, as he opened the bag and looked inside. "Yeah, we do need to talk."

Twenty minutes later, DeMarco pulled into his driveway.

"Who live here?" she asked.

"I do and you're the first person I ever brought here."

"Why?" she asked.

"I don't know, but something is telling me it's the right thing to do. Now, let's go talk about what's in this bag," he said as he got out of the car.

LaLa followed DeMarco inside. She was impressed as she looked around his crib.

"Sit, let's have a talk," DeMarco said, pointing to the couch.

Sitting down, LaLa took a deep breath as DeMarco walked into the kitchen and came back with two glasses of soda.

"Okay, what's dis?" he said, emptying the bag she gave him onto the table.

"250 grams. Now, before you say anything, let me explain somethin to you about me. I'm not as naive as it seems," LaLa said.

"So what you want from this?" he asked.

"Listen to me, DeMarco. I don't want shit back, but like I told you, I get that twice a week along with some money. Just don't hurt me; that's all I ask of you. I know shit happens—just don't let it come my way."

"What you mean, you know shit happens?" DeMarco asked.

"You're not stupid, DeMarco, you can read between the lines. I can be the best bitch you ever known or I can be the bitch you wish you never met. It's up to you, but I need to know where we stand at now before it's too late," LaLa said.

"Before *what's* too late?" he asked.

Taking a deep breath, LaLa looked right into his eyes and said, "I'm pregnant, DeMarco."

"What did you just say?" he asked, with a shocked expression on his face.

"I said I'm pregnant with your baby," she repeated.

Suddenly, DeMarco jumped up and started yelling out, "I'm having a baby!" over and over.

"Boy, be quiet," LaLa said, feeling her cheeks getting red.

"Come here with ya sexy ass!" DeMarco said, as he scooped her up and carried her to his room. "Let's bless our crib!"

He slipped his hand up her skirt until it met her pussy, moved her thong over, and started playing with her clit.

"I'm having a baby," he said to himself aloud as he laid LaLa down on the bed, pulling up her skirt and removing her thong. He kissed up her thighs until his lips made it to her pussy, where he took her clit into his mouth and began sucking on it.

"Oh my God," LaLa muttered, as her legs started to shake. "I'm about to lose it, baby!" Wrapping her legs around his head, LaLa came so hard she had to ball up to stop from shaking.

"You a'ight, ma?" DeMarco asked.

"I'm better than a'ight," LaLa said with her eyes closed. "Just give me a minute."

When he noticed that she'd fallen asleep, DeMarco left to get the things that he needed to bag up the work. After twenty minutes, he returned and peeked in the room to find LaLa still in the same exact position. He stepped softly away from the door, letting her sleep in peace, then went into the kitchen and grabbed a plate.

DeMarco sat everything down on the table in the living room, turned the TV on, and got down to business.

When LaLa entered the room, she found DeMarco passed out on the couch with a plate full of bagged crack sitting on the table. She went into her backpack, pulled out a pair of gloves, and turned on the television. She sat on the edge of the couch, watching the news, as she finished bagging up for him.

"Wassup, you?" he asked, when he awakened.

Turning her head, LaLa smiled as she slid the last rock into its package. "You," she said, pulling off the gloves. She sat on DeMarco's lap and looked into his eyes. "Baby, listen, I gotta tell my mom I'm havin a kid, and when I do, she gonna go nuts and kick me out."

"Ma, did you not hear me before? This is your crib now! You ain't gotta go anywhere, you hear me? This us right here," DeMarco said, wrapping his arms around her.

"Thank you!" LaLa said with joy.

"No, thank *you* for coming into my world," DeMarco said, and kissed her.

"Why you smiling?" she asked.

"Because we 'bout to go crazy!"

CHAPTER NINE

Fucking with Uncle Bruh for only a month, DeMarco's status went through the roof for real.

"Ayo, we goin to the Q tonight. You wit it?" Chase asked DeMarco as they drove away from one of Uncle Bruh's crack houses.

"Why wouldn't I be?" he replied.

"A'ight, I'll be back to get you at like 9," Chase said as he pulled onto 118th.

DeMarco got out at his aunt's house and watched Chase drive off. Walking across the street to his whip, he thought to himself, *Tonight is gonna be insane!* DeMarco went home to chill with LaLa for a little while before he headed out again. He had a feeling this was going to be one of those nights. He grabbed the money from under his seat and lifted the shotgun he kept with the cash and went into the house.

"Wassup, sexy?" DeMarco said, sitting down on the couch next to LaLa.

"Nothin. Went to my mom's house today. She was upset just like I knew she would be, talkin all kinds of crazy shit. *Oh, that's why you ain't gonna be shit or do shit with your life,* and a whole bunch of other hurtful shit."

DeMarco could hear in her voice that she was holding back her tears, so he pulled her into him. "I got you, ma, don't even worry about nothin. We gon' get this money together."

"I'm not worried about that, it just hurts that my own mother would say some of the things that she said to me, that's all."

"Come on, ma, let's go get somethin to eat. Hopefully a good meal will make you feel better."

Around the way, Steph sat on the porch of the crack house looking at all of the fiends coming on and off the block. *Damn, this shit is popping,* she said to herself as she watched the little niggas she had serving the heads for her.

"Ayo, Steph, I'm done," one of them said as he handed her $500.

"A'ight, you go ahead and chill. Come back in a couple of hours," Steph replied, giving the little man a fifty-dollar bill.

"Good lookin," the little nigga said as he turned to leave. The look on his face suggested he knew just what he was going to do with his bread.

DeMarco pulled up in front of his aunt's crib where Money and Tonya were sitting on the porch.

"If it ain't Ms. Never Around No More," Tonya said to LaLa as she stepped out of the car.

"Trick, don't even go there," LaLa shot back, and they both started laughing.

"Chase just left and said he'll be right back. He had to go to his crib," Money told DeMarco.

"A'ight, baby, I'll see you later," LaLa said and kissed DeMarco before walking around the car to the driver's side. "Money, I'm gonna spend some time wit my girl," LaLa said. "While people ain't hoggin it all up," she continued with a smile.

"All Tonya needs is a hug. Come here." DeMarco held his arms open wide as he walked over to her.

"Boy, move with ya silly self," Tonya said and pushed his arms away, then got into the car and closed the door.

"You good, baby?" LaLa asked.

"Yeah, I'm . . ." DeMarco started to say, but stopped when he remembered his gun was under the seat. Opening the back door, he reached his hand under the seat and pulled his gun out, trying his best to keep Tonya from seeing it. "Matter of fact, I'm good now." He tucked his heat on his hip and gave LaLa another kiss.

"See you later, sexy," she said.

Stepping back, DeMarco watched as they pulled off. "Roll up, cuz!" he called out to Money as he walked back to the porch.

Two blunts later, DeMarco was feeling nice as Chase arrived at the house. "You comin with us, cuz?" he asked Money.

"Yeah, fuck it. Where y'all going?"

"The Q Club." After DeMarco lit another blunt, they were on their way.

DeMarco noticed the long line in front of the club as they approached it.

"Damn, it's mad bitches out tonight," Money said as he rolled down the window.

Chase noticed his uncle's BMW and pulled up a few feet behind it. He turned the car off and they got out.

"Ayo, I ain't tryna wait in this long-ass line," Money said.

"Wait, what's that?" Chase said as he walked right up to the door.

"Chase, my man! What's good?" the bouncer said, giving him a pound.

"Ain't shit, Ronnie, how is it lookin in there?"

"Like always, bitches wall to wall." Ronnie laughed and stepped to the side to let Chase, DeMarco, and Money enter the club.

"Oh yeah, that's Bruh's nephew DeMarco right there. Remember that face," Chase said and kept it moving, as DeMarco gave Ronnie a pound. No pat-down or anything.

Stepping into the club, DeMarco saw what Ronnie meant about chicks being wall to wall, because everywhere he looked he saw groups of young women wearing damn near nothing.

"Now we talkin," Chase said over the noise as he made his way through the club.

Spotting Uncle Bruh in the VIP section, Chase headed that way, followed by DeMarco and Money. Chase gave the bouncer at the ropes a pound and they were all let through.

Uncle Bruh had the section locked down. The music could be heard, but you didn't have to yell at the top of your lungs to communicate.

"I see it's already poppin in here," Chase said as he gave Uncle Bruh a pound.

"You know it goes down in here." Uncle Bruh slapped a chick standing next to him on her ass. "Nephews, wassup?" he said to DeMarco and Money.

"That bottle," DeMarco said, picking up the Moët from the table.

"Yeah, drink till you can't, open bar tonight." Uncle Bruh slid his hand under the same chick he had slapped on the ass.

Drinking and smoking, DeMarco found that he couldn't stay seated. He told Money he was going to hit the dance floor and walked out into the crowded club. The DJ threw on that Uncle Luke joint and the girls started going crazy. Getting pushed against the wall by some brown-skinned chick who started pressing her ass against him, DeMarco was feeling himself.

The next couple of hours flew by. At some point De-Marco looked at his watch and saw that it was near 3 in the morning. *Damn*, he said to himself as he made his way back to the VIP area. Catching eyes with Tiffany's sister Sharon, DeMarco wasn't paying attention to where he was going and bumped into some dude, causing him to drop his drink. "My fault, fam," DeMarco said to homeboy.

"Nigga, watch where the fuck you goin!"

"Like I said, my fault, fam!" DeMarco snapped back, and started walking by, but could only take a few steps because another guy stepped in front of him.

"Ayo, you owe my man another drink," the dude said, with a stern tone.

Trying to avoid a problem, DeMarco said, "I can do that. Matter of fact, get a drink for you, ya boy, and whoever else you wit. Tell the bartender that Bruh sent you." DeMarco then tried to step around the guy.

Always on alert, even though it didn't look like he was, Uncle Bruh had been watching his nephew closely to see if he was a hothead. He didn't need those types of people around his team. When he saw DeMarco point to the bar, Uncle Bruh knew he was trying to resolve the problem without it getting out of hand.

"Chase, Money," Uncle Bruh only said once, getting up and heading out of the VIP section, all while keeping his eye on DeMarco.

Not needing to know what was up, Chase got up from between the two girls he was with, touched his hip to make sure his pistol was ready, then followed Uncle Bruh. Money was moving a little slower because he was off to the side getting his dick sucked by some light-skinned chick. He pushed her head back with one hand and tucked his joint back in with the other, then silently stepped past shorty as he went to catch up with Chase and his uncle.

Meanwhile, back a couple of feet from the VIP section, DeMarco stood looking at the guy and his friend.

"Fam, I don't want no beef with you, son, but you standing here grillin me when you got a free drink at the bar. Who does that?" DeMarco tried to step around him again, but the guy kept blocking him. DeMarco was starting to get irritated. "Nigga, I don't give a fuck about you gettin mad pussy, but save that shit for the bitch that had you," he said.

Before Uncle Bruh could intervene, DeMarco had his gun out and pressed against the guy's forehead.

"Pussy, I'll leave you dead right here," DeMarco warned.

"Hold up, nephew, easy now. It's ain't the time or place for this," Uncle Bruh said, then moved out of the way. DeMarco immediately cracked the guy across the face with his gun, dropping him to the ground. Then he started kicking the guy, who balled up in the fetal position. Lost in rage, DeMarco didn't even notice that the music had stopped and everybody was looking at him stomping the dude out. Chase, meanwhile, was backing down his boys.

"That's enough, nephew," Uncle Bruh said, grabbing DeMarco and pulling him toward the door as everyone got out of their way. Money and Chase followed. "Yo, Chase, take Money home and I'll holla at you in the a.m."

When they reached his car, Uncle Bruh waited for DeMarco to get in. He felt his nephew could fight, but he wasn't a gun buster. DeMarco was just standing there looking back at the club. Uncle Bruh saw the guy and his friend coming out, then all he heard was, *Boom boom*

boom boom boom! DeMarco was letting shots fly at the club doors.

Shocked and surprised by his nephew, he couldn't move for a moment, then snapped back into reality. "Boy, get the fuck in the car!" he yelled as he leaned over and pulled DeMarco's shirt as hard as he could.

DeMarco jumped into the car and slammed the door as his uncle pulled off.

Uncle Bruh pulled into the driveway of his crib forty minutes later.

"Yo, unc, why you takin me here?"

"'Cause you need to cool off," he replied.

DeMarco stepped through the front door and walked into the kitchen, then pulled out the Dutch he had in his pocket. "Fuck!" he muttered when he realized it was broken.

"I'll give you a Dutch if I can smoke wit you," De-Marco heard from behind him. Turning around, he saw Mia standing there in a pair of boy shorts and a tank top.

Damn, her little ass is bad, DeMarco thought to himself. "I hope you got more than one," he said out loud.

"We can't smoke out here, so you gotta come in my room. My sister doesn't smoke," Mia said.

As she walked up the stairs, he couldn't stop looking at her ass hanging out of the bottom of her shorts. Opening the second door off to the right, Mia stood there until DeMarco moved past her. She closed the door behind him.

"Sorry my room is a little messy," she said as she slid

her feet out of her slippers. She sat down on the bed and turned on the TV with the remote control. "I don't have any chairs in here because I usually don't let people in my room, so you gonna have to sit up here. Just take your shoes off." She passed a Dutch to DeMarco.

He kicked off his sneakers and sat down next to her, then went to work cracking the Dutch and rolling it.

After three blunts back to back, DeMarco rested on his elbows high as fuck, watching the movie *Juice*. He wasn't paying Mia any mind when she slid off her tank top, exposing her nice golden-brown titties. He felt her moving around behind him as she slid off her boy shorts and started rubbing on her clit. She laid there with her legs wide open, sticking two of her fingers in and out her pussy. Now that she had his attention, she pulled her fingers out and then stuck them back in. He felt his dick getting hard.

"Ever since the first day I saw you, I wanted you to fuck me every way possible. I don't want no lovey-dovey shit. If you got a girl, you can save that for her. If I'm right—and I think I am from the looks of it—you are holdin down there. I want you to fuck me any and every-where you want," she said, licking her lips.

Never one to turn down pussy from a bad-ass bitch, DeMarco stood up and took off all his clothes until he was standing there naked and rock hard. "Come and wrap those Asian lips around this dick," DeMarco said, holding his dick in his hand.

Crawling over to him, Mia grabbed the base of his dick while she licked up and down the shaft. Then she took him in her mouth and attempted to deep throat his dick.

Wrapping her long hair in his hand, DeMarco kept her head still as he face-fucked her, making her gag as he went in and out. A few more minutes of that and De-Marco was ready to kill her pussy. Pushing her back onto the bed, he got down on his knees, spread her legs damn near a full split, and then stuck his dick deep in her.

"Oh shit!" Mia yelled as DeMarco hit the bottom of her pussy. "Fuck me like we porn stars!" She grabbed her own legs and pulled them even farther apart.

Getting in the position like he was about to do a push-up, DeMarco started pounding on Mia's pussy like he was trying to knock another hole in her.

"Ohhh yesss, yesss, fuck it, fuck, fuck, fuck! Damn, boy!" she screamed.

Rising to his knees, DeMarco put one of her legs on his shoulder, lifted her off the bed, and started bouncing away. From both legs on his shoulders to doggy style, he fucked Mia every way he knew and even made up some new positions.

Back with her legs on his shoulders, DeMarco felt himself building up to cum as he pounded on Mia's pussy extra hard, causing her to yell out, "Oh my goodness, I'm fucking cumming!"

DeMarco kept going until he couldn't take it anymore. Pulling out, he jerked his dick off with his right hand as he pulled Mia's face in front of him by her hair, then came all over her face.

Taking the head of his dick in her mouth, Mia sucked out every drop before she curled up in a ball, shaking.

"You got my pussy on fire. Thank you!" she said before she fell out.

Laughing, DeMarco put his clothes back on, pulled the covers over her, grabbed another Dutch, and left the room.

Weeks had passed since the club incident and business was good for DeMarco on both sides. Sitting back in his crib, DeMarco couldn't lie: he liked having LaLa around.

"Wassup, sexy?" he said as she stood in front of him with her shirt hitched up.

Having developed the habit of watching the news every morning since LaLa moved in, DeMarco pulled her on his lap and turned the TV on.

"A body was found around 2 a.m. on Jamaica Avenue," the reporter said.

DeMarco started absently rubbing between LaLa's legs, but she slapped his hand when something on the TV caught her attention.

"Yesterday in upstate New York, a police officer was killed when he responded to a silent alarm at a jewelry store. A shoot-out erupted as two criminals fired, killing the officer and the store security guard. Sometime this morning, police apprehended two suspects. Their names are Johnny Jones and Nicky Costolow," the reporter said as a picture of Lil' Nicky appeared on the screen.

"Damn, Lil' Nicky, they gonna finish you!" DeMarco said.

"Babe, what's wrong, you know him?' LaLa asked.

"Hell yeah! We was locked up together," he replied, shaking his head.

CHAPTER TEN

"Yo, who dis?" DeMarco was standing in front of his aunt's crib.

"Wassup, you? I haven't heard from you in a while," Tiffany said.

"My fault, Tiff, I been mad busy, yo, word, but don't think I ain't been thinkin about you, ma."

"Oh yeah? So that means you can come and break me off somethin real nice. I might even have a little surprise for you," Tiffany said.

"Give me a half and I'll be through."

"A'ight, I'll see you then," she replied.

Just as DeMarco hung up, he saw Steph coming up the street. He picked up his book bag from the steps and slung it over his shoulder. "Wassup, cuz?"

"You, me, us, and money," Steph said. "I heard about the little movie scene you had at the Q Club a couple weeks ago."

"Who, me? Nah, that wasn't me, cuz," DeMarco replied with a smile.

"Um huh, don't tell me nothin," Steph said as they hit the corner of the block.

Looking around first, Steph slid the book bag off her shoulders and passed it to DeMarco as he did the same with his.

"Something's in there for you too, cuz," DeMarco said. "Speaking of which, I like the way you got them lil' niggas holdin the block down."

"Nah, I just got one open off my pussy. He controls the rest of them, and I control him," Steph replied.

"That's my cousin. I'll get wit you later, a'ight?" DeMarco turned back around and headed down the street. He hopped in his car to drop off the money he'd just gotten from Steph.

Pulling up into Tiffany's projects, DeMarco parked close to the building. He thought to take his gun, but changed his mind at the last second. He knocked on the door of her third-floor apartment and heard the locks click before the door opened.

"Damn," DeMarco said as Tiffany stood in the doorway in a pair of red heels, a black thong, and matching bra. He hugged her and grabbed her ass.

"You like that?" she asked.

"You know I do," DeMarco said, smiling.

"Well, I got something real nice for you tonight," Tiffany said as DeMarco's phone started ringing. "No, no, daddy, you all mine tonight." She led him through the apartment. "I got a couple of people I want you to meet," she said as she opened the door to her bedroom.

DeMarco stared at three chicks ass-naked on Tiffany's bed.

"This is what I do for my daddy," Tiffany said, then led DeMarco into the room and closed the door behind them.

Meanwhile across town, Uncle Bruh pulled up to his crib with a funny feeling in his stomach.

Something is off, he thought to himself as he went into the house.

"Wassup, baby, how was your day today?" he asked Meesha, who was sitting in the living room.

"Good, even though I just stayed around the house," she replied.

"Where Mia at?"

"She upstairs in her room," Meesha said. "You hungry?"

"Yeah, I could eat something," he replied.

DeMarco was laid out in the middle of Tiffany's bed with all four chicks sucking all over his body.

"Hold up, Tiff. Watch out, bet, you can't do this," a chick named Sonya said as she moved Tiffany's mouth from DeMarco's dick.

DeMarco leaned up on his elbows as Sonya straddled him. Spreading her legs wide, she grabbed DeMarco's dick and stuck it in her ass and started popping up and down like nothing he'd ever seen.

"Go Sonya, go Sonya, go Sonya!" the other chicks yelled as Sonya started bouncing even faster.

* * *

Over at Uncle Bruh's house, Chase parked his whip next to one of Uncle Bruh's BMWs, got out, walked up to the door, and then rang the bell.

"Ayo, Meesha, can you get that? It's only Chase," Uncle Bruh called out from the living room.

"What's good, big bro?" Chase said as he headed inside.

"Shit," Uncle Bruh replied.

Chase sat down as Meesha walked in with Uncle Bruh's food. "You hungry, Chase?" she asked.

"Nah, I'm good, Meesha. I just ate a little while ago."

"A'ight, I'll be upstairs if you need me, baby," she said to Uncle Bruh before kissing him and walking off.

As the two men talked about the last couple of weeks, Uncle Bruh passed a blunt to Chase.

Boom, boom, boom!

"What the fuck!" Uncle Bruh shouted and turned to the front door.

"FBI! Everybody on the fucking floor!"

Getting on their knees, Chase and Uncle Bruh just looked at each other and shook their heads.

"Time to play the game," Uncle Bruh muttered to his nephew.

At Tiffany's house, DeMarco was awakened by the sound of his phone ringing. Looking at his watch, he saw it was about 8:50. He slid out of the bed slowly so he wouldn't wake anyone up, then stood at the foot of it getting dressed while looking down at the four naked women.

"Damn," DeMarco whispered as he left the room. Getting into his car he checked his phone. He saw that he had missed a number of calls, but there were no messages.

Bumping an underground mixtape he got from his uncle, he pulled up to his crib. Not seeing the BMW, he figured LaLa wasn't home.

He took a quick shower and sat in the living room to watch TV.

"In today's news, the top story: Last night local police teamed up with the FBI and took down one of the biggest drug dealers in Queens, thirty-nine-year-old Brian Biggit, along with one of his top lieutenants. No other arrests have been made at this time."

DeMarco was punching in Uncle Bruh's number when his phone started ringing.

"Yo, who dis?"

"Come to the house," Aunt V. said and immediately hung up.

DeMarco jumped off the couch, grabbed his keys from the table, and flew out the door. Fifteen minutes later, he pulled up in front of his aunt's house, noticing a black Range Rover sitting in front of the crib.

CHAPTER ELEVEN

After getting word from his uncle, DeMarco was in charge of collecting the money that niggas owed and giving it to Meesha. Knowing he needed a little help holding down his uncle's few blocks, DeMarco had Uncle Bruh's shooter, Killer C take care of it. Three weeks had passed since Uncle Bruh and Chase were arrested and they still didn't have a bail amount set. DeMarco went by to check on Meesha at least once a day and to roll around and get sweaty with Mia.

With LaLa's stomach getting bigger by the day, he tried not to stay out all night anymore, but you know what they say: when you marry the streets, you marry the bitch for life. Things were running smoothly at first with Uncle Bruh locked up, but slowly that started to change.

DeMarco and Killer C went through 127th and Merrick to check on the block. When they pulled up in front,

Ten-Ten—one of the little niggas who was loyal to his uncle—was standing outside.

"Ten-Ten, what's good?" DeMarco said, getting out of his Legend.

"Same shit, yo, but wassup with unc?"

"Shit looking crazy still, but we just gotta wait and see what happens. But yo, who them niggas over there?" DeMarco pointed at three dudes up the block on the other side of the street.

"I was gonna ask you if you sent some niggas this way. They been up there for a couple days," Ten-Ten said.

"Hell nah, I ain't send them," DeMarco said as he walked off toward the guys. "Can I help you, fellas?" De-Marco asked as he approached.

"Nah, we good," one of them said.

"Not here you ain't good," Killer C called over.

DeMarco knew sooner or later niggas would try to move on these blocks now that the streets knew his uncle was locked up. Without another word, he pulled out his gun and smacked the closest dude across the face, dropping him. Killer C backed the other two up against the wall.

"Nigga, ain't shit change because my uncle locked up, we still got this block! If I catch any of you tryna move on any block of mines, niggas is dead," DeMarco warned, then turned and walked away. He had a feeling this might not be the last time he'd have to check niggas. Back at his whip he said, "Ayo, Ten-Ten, if those niggas show up again, call me right away, a'ight?"

"A'ight, I got you."

DeMarco pulled off, leaving Ten-Ten on the block.

"You know they gonna come back, right?" Killer C said.

"I'm thinking that, which is why we gonna play the blocks close—especially that one—for a couple days. I'll meet you out here every night at 10 for the rest of this week."

"A'ight," Killer C replied.

"I'm about to go check on shorty, so I'll get up wit you later," DeMarco said as they pulled up to his aunt's crib.

"Handle ya business, my nigga, and I'll get up wit you later." Killer C gave DeMarco a pound before he got out of the car.

Taking a deep breath, DeMarco thought about his uncle as he pulled off.

It was a hot summer night. DeMarco and Killer C were outside on the block doing what they did best. There were fiends everywhere and money was pouring in like rain.

DeMarco noticed two women coming down the street dressed like hookers. One of them walked up to him and asked, "You got a light?"

DeMarco told Killer C to help her out as he stepped to the back of the car where the hammer was at; something about the situation felt funny. As he bent over reaching into the vehicle, he heard his boy say, "Oh shit, this nigga got a gun!"

When DeMarco stood up, the window of the car

shattered. Ducking back down low, he saw his boy run toward where he knew the other gun was. DeMarco made a move to run, but suddenly felt a pain in his left leg. Hearing shot after shot, he dipped back to give himself a second to think. Then, he was running and ducking while shooting back like he was a character in *Scarface*. He leaned against the side of a parked car, trying to catch his breath and slow his heart, which felt like it was in a drag race. As more shots flew, he looked across the street and saw Killer C firing.

"We gotta get up outta here before the cops come!" DeMarco yelled to Killer C.

They jumped into a rental car they left parked around the corner and checked DeMarco's leg. They decided to go to the hospital, but left before the doctor came to ask any questions.

After that incident, DeMarco knew he had to get a stronger team. Killer C was known for laying his gun game down, but that wasn't going to be enough. The block was making a lot of money and he wasn't going to give it up so easily.

He called a meeting the very next day and enlisted a notorious hustler and shooter he admired named Chief and his crew. After a few weeks of working together, it became evident that Chief's team was so strong that De-Marco had cats in every borough talking about them. If you blinked wrong, they would shoot you. Shit was getting hot and DeMarco had to figure things out, so he decided to take a trip out of town to visit a few of his cousins in North Carolina, deep inside the Dirty South.

He'd hustled down there before, so getting to the money wouldn't be a problem.

Once DeMarco reached down South, he picked up one of his country homeboys named Cash. They were going to see Michelle and one of her friends. He knew Michelle through his cousins, so he called her to slide through her house for the first time.

"Damn, boy, it took you months to come down here to my house," she said, while chewing her gum. "De-Marco, you can have a seat. I'm not gonna bite you. Y'all boys from New York are crazy!"

DeMarco sat down and looked around, while Cash went to Michelle's homegirl's house. All he could think about was how he was going to fuck her.

"I got Henny if you want some," she said.

"Yeah, I'll take some with no ice," he replied.

Michelle walked into the kitchen with her boy shorts on to make his drink. "If you want, you can chill in my room until I come in there."

DeMarco got up and headed to her room. A few minutes later he heard someone calling her name. He hopped up off her queen-size bed and looked out the window, but didn't see anyone.

Someone started calling her name again. This time it sounded like they were inside the house. DeMarco pulled out an all-black seventeen shot Glock and peeked out of the room to find three dudes coming down the hall-way. They were headed straight for the room he was in. He couldn't help but think Michelle set him up, when he noticed that one of them was a nigga named Black, who was her brother. He had robbed him for money and work a while back when he was visiting his cousins one summer. As the dude pushed the door open, DeMarco let off two shots, hitting him in the shoulder and stomach. Black hit the floor as his homeboys started firing back. DeMarco ran toward the window to try to get out, but there was another nigga standing down below. He had no option but to keep shooting.

"Let's dance, muthafuckers!" DeMarco yelled before blasting.

Across the street, Cash was chilling at Michelle's homegirl's crib.

Cash heard the shots, looked out the window, immediately got up, and grabbed his gun. He ran into Michelle's house, catching them from behind.

After they were all laid out, DeMarco and Cash hurried out of the house.

"You straight?" Cash asked as they made their way to the car.

"Yeah, man, good looking. I owe you one," DeMarco replied.

"Man, DeMarco, that shit was nothing. Let's get the fuck outta here!"

As they turned the corner, DeMarco noticed Michelle coming out of a store. He pulled up, as calm as ever.

"Wassup, ma?" he asked.

"Where you goin? Why you ain't in the house?" she asked.

"Get in the car, I gotta make a quick run," DeMarco

said softly. "Let me borrow your phone, shorty." He looked at the phone, put it on silent, stuck it in his pocket, then turned the stereo on: Mobb Deep—"Survival of the Fittest" was bumping though the speakers.

"I like this song, this shit is hot," Michelle said.

DeMarco just nodded his head as Cash passed him a blunt. Taking a pull, DeMarco thought about his next move. He felt her phone vibrating over and over in his pocket as he passed her the blunt. DeMarco knew the streets were talking, so he decided to go see his cousin a few towns over. He also knew that sooner or later Michelle would start asking questions.

Ten minutes later they pulled up to his cousin Jazz's house. DeMarco had a special way he blew his horn to let his cuz know it was him.

Jazz ran out of the house with his little brother, Rah.

"Wassup, DeMarco?" Rah said. "Nigga, when you get down here? I hope you got the good-smelling shit for us, we tryna get high too."

From the look on DeMarco's face, Jazz could tell something was wrong. "Come on in," he said.

The two men walked inside the house with Rah while Cash stayed in the car with Michelle.

"Yo, cuzzo, what's good?" Jazz asked.

DeMarco started putting Jazz and Rah onto what had just happened.

"So what's good, yo? Talk to me, what you want us to do?" Rah asked.

"I want you to hold this bitch here until I come back in a few days. But don't let her outta your sight."

Rah seemed to get a kick out of shit like this.

"Yo, come on in!" DeMarco yelled out the front door to Cash and Michelle.

DeMarco took the woman straight to the bedroom, pulled her pants down, and she fucked the shit out of him. She sucked his dick for thirty minutes straight. After he was done with her, she fell asleep and he left her in the room stretched out on the bed. He gave his cousin the look, threw $2,000 on the table, and walked out.

By morning, police were all over the place searching for DeMarco and Cash; Michelle had told one of her friends that DeMarco was coming over. Plus, the slut across the street who had been fucking Cash said she saw what happened.

DeMarco's cell was ringing off the hook.

"Where the hell you at?" his Aunt Bernice yelled into the phone. "Them people came to my house askin me where you was and somethin about you kidnappin a girl and shootin somebody! Boy, you betta not come down here wit that shit!"

DeMarco hung up on her. He was furious! *The nerve of these pussies.* Through Uncle Bruh, he had two of the best lawyers, one in New York and one in North Carolina, so going to jail was the last thing on his mind. He decided to call his older shorty named India who was a bail bondsman he fucked with. He wanted to find out what she'd heard.

"Yo, wassup, India baby? This your boy."

"Oh, wassup, Mr. Clint Eastwood shootin up houses and shit!" she yelled.

"Man, fuck all that," DeMarco countered. "What's the word out there? I heard they was lookin for me."

"Yeah, something like that," India replied with a little attitude; she knew DeMarco was fucking with another bitch.

"What you mean? Find out what's good and hit me back," DeMarco said.

"Okay, cool, I'll hit you back. Be safe and lay low, daddy."

DeMarco had family all over the South, so laying low was easy. He called up one of his other shorties and told her to meet him at a Super 8 motel.

He had to make a run before he got to the motel. As he reached his spot, he circled the block twice, moving slowly and looking at everything closely before he pulled up to his stash house. Hidden away in Piney Green, he had never taken anybody to this place that he only used when he was in town. DeMarco hit the code on the alarm, stepped inside, immediately opened the stash that he had in the floor, and counted out a quick $50,000. His ringing phone interrupted him.

"Yo, yo, hello?"

"Why haven't you been answerin your phone? This my fourth time callin you," India said.

"Wassup, baby?" DeMarco said softly.

"This is the deal: I'm not sayin you do or you don't, but if you know where that girl is, you need someone to take her to your lawyer to sign an affidavit sayin you didn't kidnap her. Also, quiet as kept, I heard you could beat the shoot-out in the house because they came in on you. One of the guys is talkin already though. He told the whole story. So don't forget: if you can find that girl, get her to go to your lawyer. Oh, and tell her to say she left you in the house and she locked all the doors."

"Okay, cool. Thanks, baby," DeMarco replied, then grabbed his two guns and his bulletproof vest. He had always felt that he'd rather get caught with it than without it.

"Where you been? Do you know how long I been out here? And why are you dressed like that?" she asked when he arrived at the Super 8.

DeMarco kissed her on the cheek. "Take it easy, shorty."

"Where is my Gucci bag, playboy?" she asked, while holding her hand out.

"Yo, take this $2,000 and this bag for me," he replied.

"Where are you goin?" she asked, with a frustrated look on face.

"I gotta bust a quick move, but do me a favor—first thing in the mornin, take the bag to my Aunt Sheena." One thing about his Aunt Sheena: she didn't play when it came to DeMarco. For one, his mother had died when he was younger and she made sure her nephew was always in good hands. However you put it, she was on his side.

"Word," she replied.

"Shorty, don't forget." He looked at her with a serious face, then kissed her goodbye and got into the car to head back to his cousin's spot.

When he knocked on the door, Rah immediately opened it with concern and said, "Wassup, nigga, you good?"

"Hell yeah, we good. Wassup with shorty?" DeMarco asked.

"Oh, she good. She doesn't even have a clue, my nigga. We kept her high off that fire you gave us. Come on, shorty, Cash, and Jazz is in the backyard blazin up. You came just in time."

When Michelle saw DeMarco her face lit up. "Where you been?" she asked. "Do you have my phone?"

"Oh, I had to make a quick run, but check this out, let me holla at you." DeMarco gave her the rundown on what he needed her to do.

Michelle just sat there, stuck like she was dreaming. She was at a loss for words, hoping her brother wasn't hurt badly, but at the same time, she didn't want DeMarco to think she'd set him up. She would do whatever he asked to prove that she was loyal: "Okay, no problem. I got you, baby," she said in a sincere tone.

Later that night, DeMarco met with Cash at a motel to talk business. As they were talking, the phone rang and an unknown number showed on the screen of DeMarco's phone.

"Yo, who dis?"

"Yo, nigga, this me—Jazz. We took care of that. Everything cool."

"A'ight, but whose number is dis?" DeMarco asked.

"Come on, we was taught by the best. This a pay phone number. We got you," Jazz replied.

"A'ight, let me holla at shorty."

"Hello, daddy," Michelle said with her country accent.

"Wassup, girl? What you doin?"

"Shit, I'm ready to see you again. I wanted to ask you if I could bring two of my friends with me."

DeMarco got quiet for a minute, but he knew Michelle was trying to show him her loyalty and he was thinking that dick was power.

"So who are these girls?" DeMarco asked.

"Oh, it's two of my best friends, Tia and Kee-Kee."

"Okay, Michelle, check this out. Don't call 'em though, just go to they house and pick 'em up," he said.

"Okay, cool," Michelle said with a big smile on her face. "I love you, daddy."

"Yeah, right, you love this dick! Now don't forget what I said," DeMarco replied.

"I know, I got you, daddy."

"A'ight, put Jazz on the phone."

"Yo, wassup, boy?" Jazz said.

"Yeah, she talkin about bringin her homegirls wit y'all to meet up with me. I told her it was cool."

"Yeah, a'ight. I hope you can trust her," Jazz said.

"If this bitch try anything, she outta here," DeMarco said and hung up the phone. "Come on, my nigga, we outta here. We gotta get some new rooms." He grabbed a towel and started wiping everything down. He didn't want to leave any evidence of being there.

"Fuck you doin?" Cash asked.

"See, that's the problem wit you niggas. Y'all don't think about fingerprints and shit. Well I do!"

"Come on, we out then," Cash said, shaking his head.

After DeMarco was satisfied that the room was free of fingerprints, they exited.

"Man, I need a drink or somethin," Cash said.

"Shit, me too, yo," DeMarco replied. "I got a lil' spot on the low that I used to go down to where a lot of classic old heads be at."

"A'ight, let's get it then." They hopped in the car and made their way over to the bar, which was crowded. Most of the patrons were older, with a few young people scattered throughout.

"May I help you guys?" The fine-ass blond waitress smirked while looking them up and down.

"You can start by givin me your number," DeMarco replied.

"You so crazy!" she said with a giggle. "What can I get you to drink?"

"Can I have two White Russians with no ice, and some buffalo wings with french fries? Also, let me get a Sprite with lemon," DeMarco said.

"What can I get for you, young man?" she asked Cash.

"Oh, I'll have the same thing he ordered."

"Okay, give me a few and I'll be back with your drinks," she said before walking away.

"Shorty got the Pamela Anderson look," Cash said.

"Shit, you ain't lyin. I need that on the team. By the way, have you been checkin on things?" DeMarco didn't play when it came to money.

"Yeah, everything is cool. But I forgot to tell you, your man Killer C from up top called last night."

"Word? Why the hell you ain't tell me?"

"Shit, my nigga, it was mad late. It slipped my mind."

"Yo, you got a clean phone on you?" DeMarco asked.

"You know I do." Cash reached in his pocket and passed the phone to DeMarco, who immediately got up from the table and walked outside to call Killer C.

"Wassup?" DeMarco said.

"You know me. I'm up here makin it do what it do, my nigga. When you comin back up this way? I need you soon. Plus, your man Skip keep askin about you."

"Word? That nigga home? My nigga, get his number for me," DeMarco said. "But let me put you onto what's been goin on down here."

Killer C just stayed quiet while DeMarco filled him in as much as he could in code since they were on the phone; Killer C couldn't believe what he was hearing. He was on fire like a heat wave or a bomb waiting to explode. After his uncle got locked up, DeMarco and Killer C had developed a bond that no one could ever break.

"Yo, DeMarco, I told you to let me come down there with you! Yo, I would've turned that whole town upside down!" Killer C yelled through the phone.

"Nah, my nigga. Everything is good. I got this, plus I need you to keep shit tight up there for me. Trust, I got this."

"Let me know your shooters on deck."

"A'ight, bet, and don't forget to get Skip's number for me and tell Bizzy to get at me. I heard he just came home too," DeMarco said.

"A'ight, I got you, my nigga, be safe out there."

"Next time, no questions asked, I'm there. So I'm about to be out," DeMarco said.

"When you comin back up?"

"Come on, yo. You know I don't kiss and tell," De-Marco replied.

"A'ight, whatever, man. I'll holla at you later," Killer C said.

"Do that." DeMarco ended the call and walked back to the table where Cash was waiting impatiently.

"Damn, nigga. What, you got lost or somethin?" Cash said as soon as DeMarco sat back down. "Shit, it's old school in here for real—donkeys all over the place."

"I told you, this my spot. My sister put me onto this joint. This spot is the shit." DeMarco watched the waitress making her way over to the table.

"Here are your drinks," she said.

Cracking joke after joke, DeMarco and Cash sat laughing and eating. But the whole time DeMarco was saying to himself, *I don't know what it is, but it's somethin about this nigga.* He felt his waistband to make sure his nine was ready.

"Yo, I'm tryna get me one of these old head joints," Cash said as he sipped on his drink. "They say those are the ones to have."

"Yeah, that's what I heard," DeMarco muttered back.

The waitress returned with the check and slipped DeMarco her number. He left her five one hundred–dollar bills and walked away from the table.

"Yo, DeMarco, I think this is Jazz and them calling me," Cash said as they were leaving.

"Oh, word? So pick it up."

Cash did as instructed.

"Yo, this Jazz. Where y'all niggas at?"

"Hold on, my nigga." Cash passed the phone to DeMarco.

"Wassup, Jazz?"

"You tell me what you want us to do."

"Meet us by the Fairfield Inn hotel," DeMarco said.

"A'ight, bet," Jazz replied.

CHAPTER TWELVE

"Cash, go inside and get two rooms, but make sure they attached in case these chicks try to pull some funny shit," DeMarco said.

"A'ight, cool."

"Wassup, ladies?" DeMarco said as Jazz and Rah arrived with Michelle, Kee-Kee, and Tia. The girls were clearly excited to be around DeMarco, as if they could see dollar signs.

"Yo, DeMarco, let me holla at you," Rah said.

"Yo, what's good, Rah?"

"Nah, everything good, but just to let you know, these chicks are ready. You know I play stupid, but I keep my ears open. I overheard them say they would do anything to be around you," Rah said. "And that's beautiful, because we just don't want any kind of bitches around us, fat asses or not. Yo, a nigga tired, but I got to go find somethin to eat, plus Jazz is tryna find some bitches for the night."

"What's wrong wit Tia and Kee-Kee?" DeMarco asked.

"Shit, I tried to holla at them, but they both said they wanted you."

"Wow, gonna see about that."

"Jazz, let's go get something to eat," Rah said.

"Fuck that, I'm goin too," Cash said, as he followed Jazz and Rah out the door.

DeMarco stayed at the hotel with the ladies.

"Damn, daddy, you don't have nothin to smoke?" Michelle asked.

"Shit, are The Fat Boys fat?" DeMarco said with a laugh. "Open the bottom drawer, I got all types of good ass bud in there."

The women were staring at DeMarco as if he were a bite to eat.

"Turn on the TV or somethin. Y'all acting like he's gonna bite y'all or some shit," Michelle said.

Kee-Kee opened her Louis Vuitton suitcase and pulled out two big-ass bottles of Hennessy. Michelle took both of the girls into the bathroom and started schooling them.

"Listen, bitches, we gonna party like rock stars and don't be asking a lot of questions," she said.

"Girl, we know that," Kee-Kee replied.

"A'ight, on the count of three: one, two, three . . . We in dis bitch!"

DeMarco was sitting on the chair like a don watching the women.

"Damn, daddy, give me some of your blunt," Michelle said.

"Shit, if you know like I know, you better roll up your own blunt. Matter of fact, all y'all need to roll up your own shit," DeMarco said. He wanted to make sure everybody was high.

"Daddy, we're gonna take a quick shower, so we can get nice and fresh for you."

"Shit, ain't nothin wrong with that. Make yourself at home."

"Kee-Kee, can you pass me my panties out of my bag?" Tia called out.

"You don't need any panties, don't you know who we wit? This is New York's Finest himself," Michelle said as she headed to the bathroom with her glass of Henny.

Ten minutes later, the girls hopped out of the shower looking like three porn stars. DeMarco had a fetish for baby oil on fat asses; his dick stood up like an arrow.

"Girl, look at his tattoos," Kee-Kee whispered to Tia.

"So this is what we gonna to do for you, daddy. We gonna play doctor and fix your problem," Michelle said as she started rubbing baby oil all over DeMarco's body.

"What y'all lookin at me for? Y'all not gonna help me?"

"Hell yeah," Kee-Kee said. She was always down for whatever.

"Here, pour some in my hand," Tia said, then started rubbing DeMarco's dick and the top of his stomach. Michelle began sucking it and Kee-Kee was licking the side of it like a lollipop. After fifteen minutes of them tag-teaming his dick, DeMarco laid Michelle out and began fucking her pussy slowly.

"Give it to me, daddy. Give it to me harder. Show these bitches why you my daddy," she moaned.

"Come on, give me some!" Kee-Kee couldn't wait any longer.

"Pass me that cup." DeMarco took two more sips and then started fucking Kee-Kee. As soon as DeMarco put his dick in her, she started cumming.

"You like that?" he said, laughing as he glanced over at Tia, who was looking a little lost. "Oh, you thought I was gonna forget about you? Hell no I wasn't," he said to her.

Tia wanted DeMarco to hit it from the back while Michelle kissed her and Kee-Kee ate her pussy.

"This what I'm talkin about," DeMarco said, feeling like he was in heaven.

Michelle was showing him she was a real bitch, and her homegirls were down by all means.

DeMarco soon had Tia damn near going through the headboard.

"Okay, enough, I can't take it nomore," Tia said as she came all over DeMarco's dick.

Jazz, Cash, and Rah were in the club popping bottles like they'd won the championship game. Chicks from all the local towns were all over them.

"Damn, Jazz, this is the life," Rah said to his older brother.

"We gotta get money like DeMarco and Cash," Jazz replied while getting a lap dance.

"Man, I'm tryna fuck somethin!"

"Man, you don't know where you at? Follow me." Cash took Jazz and Rah to the Boom Boom Room. "Which one do you want? Black, Chinese, white, or Indian?"

"I want her," Rah said, pointing to a white chick.

"Can I help you, sweetheart? What would you like?"

"Shit, I'll start off with a blow job." Rah couldn't believe what money could buy.

"Wow, we gotta try that again tomorrow," Rah said when they exited the club an hour later. "But now we gotta check on DeMarco."

DeMarco and the girls were out like a light when Cash and Rah knocked on the door to make sure everything was good. DeMarco woke up only to say that he would holla at them in the morning, then went back to sleep.

The boys stayed up all night talking about their episodes.

"Man, we better get some sleep. You know that nigga DeMarco is gonna wake up on some other shit," Cash said.

The next morning, DeMarco showered and brushed his teeth before agreeing to take everyone to the mall.

"Light that up, Michelle, and pull something out for me to wear today. I'm tryna do the Polo sweatsuit with these Jordan's," DeMarco said.

They bought so much shit at the mall that even the security guards were following them around the place like they were rock stars.

Kee-Kee whispered to the girls, "Shit, this is the life I wanna live."

Michelle looked back at the girls and said, "I told you! We in dis bitch!"

"Daddy, check this out. Tia and Kee-Kee know these guys they fuckin from Miami who be holdin a lot of bricks," Michelle said.

The girls couldn't wait to get back to the room to put DeMarco on to some niggas they knew who were trafficking drugs from Miami to North Carolina. Leaving DeMarco was the last thing on their minds; they were all in it for the long haul.

"When they pick up, how much coke they got and where the stash houses at?" DeMarco asked.

After the girls broke it down to him, he couldn't believe how many bricks they said the niggas had. He thought surely they must have a Mexican connect. Once De-Marco had the info, he devised a plan that was sure to work. "Y'all know what to do, so don't fuck this up! I'll call y'all when we ready."

Later that week, Rah and Jazz jumped on the highway and met DeMarco with his team. Just as planned, they ran down on the stash houses while the dudes were across town and caught them for ten bricks.

As soon as DeMarco got back from the jux, Tia's phone started ringing.

"Hello, who dis?"

"Have you seen my crazy-ass sista?" Black yelled into the phone.

"Hold on," she said, passing the phone to Michelle.

"Where the fuck you at? I almost got killed because

you fuckin wit that nigga DeMarco at your house!" he screamed.

"DeMarco?" Michelle said.

"A'ight, keep playin stupid. Where the fuck you at? I'm not askin you again."

"I'm out wit Tia and Kee-Kee. I'll meet you at ma's house," she replied.

"Yeah, well, hurry up, because you got niggas thinkin that nigga kidnapped you or somethin."

"Boy, bye. Ain't nobody kidnapped me. I'm on my way."

From the look on Michelle's face, DeMarco knew she wasn't going to set him up. Plus, she'd just put him on to ten bricks.

"So what you want me to do?" she asked.

"This what I'm gonna do. I'm gonna drop y'all off at Kee-Kee's house and when y'all get finished, hit me up. Remember, y'all on the team now, so silence is golden," DeMarco said.

When they pulled up to Michelle's mother's house, her brother and his whole team were waiting on her. Michelle took a deep breath and got out of the car.

"Where you been? I told you stop fucking with Kee-Kee and Tia!"

Smack.

Black hit Michelle so hard she saw birds and stars at the same time. She kneeled down because she thought she was going to pass out.

"If I was gonna help you, I'm definitely not helpin your punk ass now!" she shouted.

"Look what this nigga did to me! And he shot Man-Man. You better help us find that nigga."

"I don't know where he at," she said.

"Shoot, that's the problem with y'all lil' fast-ass girls, lettin niggas come from out of town and take over shit."

"Come on, girl." Michelle jumped into Tia's car and they quickly drove off.

"I hate that nigga," Michelle said, as she wiped her tears away.

About a week later, DeMarco's phone rang. "Yo, wassup?" he asked.

"DeMarco, where you been? I called you over a week ago already. I got it set up wit your lawyer for you to turn yourself in," India said.

"Turn myself in?" he said, as he thought about not getting out if his escape from Tryon showed up.

"You're my baby. You know I ain't gonna leave you in there, plus I'm not trying to lose that good ol' dick. They're gonna have your bail at $150,000. I already spoke to your aunt, she's gonna sign for you and we'll get you right out."

"So when is all of this supposed to happen?" DeMarco asked.

"I tell you what, I'll call your lawyer and hit you back."

CHAPTER THIRTEEN

I n no time, DeMarco was back on the streets just like India said. He felt untouchable since the escape didn't show up and it was his first time getting locked up out of state.

Jazz and Rah stared at the bricks all night like they were presents under a Christmas tree. DeMarco's phone started ringing; it was Michelle.

"Daddy, where you at? Are you a'ight? I was calling you all day."

"I'm good. I had to turn myself in for that bullshit."

"Can you believe that bitch-ass brotha of mines had the nerve to slap me in front of his pussy-ass friends?" she said, with anger in her voice.

"He did *what?* Oh, don't worry, he really fucked up now."

"Come get us, daddy, I'm at Kee-Kee's aunt's house."

"Cool, I got you. I'll be there in a few minutes."

But DeMarco first had to stop and check on his Auntie Sheena.

"Boy, is you a'ight?" Aunt Sheena asked, as he walked through the door.

"Yeah, I'm good."

"I have been waiting to see you. I was just telling your uncle that you have to be careful down here."

Auntie Sheena was from New York too, but had moved to North Carolina years earlier.

"Well, some boy keep callin you named Skip or somethin like that. And what did I tell you about givin people my number? You know you don't live here?!"

Auntie Sheena didn't play about people coming or calling her house. Her favorite line was, *Ain't gonna have nobody run up in my house, but if they do, I got somethin for their ass.* Auntie Sheena was gangster!

"A'ight, I got you," DeMarco said.

"I'm dead-ass serious, boy, don't play with me."

DeMarco gave his aunt a hug, kiss, and passed her a knot as big as Patrick Ewing's left foot. Then he picked up his phone and dialed Skip's number.

"Who dis? DeMarco?"

"And you know," DeMarco replied.

"Man, I heard about you way upstate! Boy, you the talk of the jails. Niggas said you doin your thing. When you comin to get a nigga?" Skip asked.

"Me and my niggas got this shit on lock-down here!"

"I want in!"

"Did you see Bizzy?"

"Yeah, I saw him last week at parole."

"Yeah, niggas still on papers?"

"Man, fuck all that, I'm down there. Them niggas gotta catch me if they can."

"Okay, get at Bizzy and I'm gonna tell Killer C to put you on a plane tomorrow."

"A'ight, bet, we there."

DeMarco needed real niggas with him because he knew that from now on, there was no turning back.

The next day they caught the plane and arrived in North Carolina a couple hours later.

"Damn, my nigga, it looks crazy down here."

"Shit, did they starve you in the joint? You skinny as fuck," DeMarco said to Skip.

"DeMarco, you know I don't get fat. I've been skinny all my life."

"What's the verdict, Bizzy?" DeMarco asked.

"Man, you know me."

Bizzy wasn't the type who talked a lot, but he was down for whatever. DeMarco started to put them onto what was going on and how things were run down there. "I got a spot where y'all can rest. Tomorrow will be y'all first day on the job."

The money was coming so fast that Skip and Bizzy had to buy a notepad to keep track of the numbers they were bringing in.

"Who are these pretty young ladies?" Skip asked DeMarco.

"These are my besties. If you fuck with them, you got problems with me."

"Nah, I'm just saying, they are fine as wine. How y'all doin?"

They just looked at him and rolled their eyes.

The streets were definitely talking now. The whole area knew about DeMarco and his crew, and to top it off, he had half the niggas and bitches in pocket. The clubs wouldn't jump off until DeMarco and his crew showed up. Bottle after bottle, they were buying it up. Sometimes the club owners had to go to other venues in the area to get more bottles. Those half-ass hustlers didn't have shit on these Queens niggas. They even had police trying to get on their team. See, Skip was always a hustler and that was right up DeMarco's alley. He came down with that dub-up shit: when you bought a hundred, he would give you two hundred, so he changed the game and this made him that nigga. Skip had a chick named Kai from New York who taught him the game for real, but she had to cut him off—she said he wasn't ready for a real chick like her. Man, that chick was a keeper! The nigga lost his mind fucking up with her. One time he lied and told her he'd bought her a ring. DeMarco ran to Zale's Jewelers and bought it for her because he knew that with her around, Skip would be on his A-game.

Niggas don't miss a good thing until it's gone, DeMarco thought to himself. *Shit, I'm glad I gotta chick like that, don't no shorty come before LaLa.* Ain't nothing better than a real bitch. Skip couldn't wait to go back to New York and show the hood how he came up, but DeMarco had him chill because Skip was his man and he didn't want him to get knocked.

DeMarco and his crew started getting larger than large. Niggas were scared to fuck with anybody else but them. If they didn't have the work right then, they would wait for them to get it. All the niggas who grew up in the area were sick besides the ones down with DeMarco and his crew; the fiends and young hustlers wouldn't buy weight from nobody but them.

Black couldn't stand DeMarco. He was taking money from them and he had popped him and his man. So, he decided to call a meeting with the local hustlers that weren't fucking with DeMarco and his crew.

"Here's how it's gonna go down," Black explained. "We got to get this nigga DeMarco and his guys out our town. We gonna start robbin all of this nigga's workers, and nobody gettin work from nobody else except me. But give me a week," he concluded as he and Man-Man walked away with two big-ass niggas.

No questions asked, Man-Man knew just what to do. He gassed the black van up and jumped on the highway. Black had some cousins from Connecticut who were gangsters.

After a long drive, they finally made it to Connecticut and pulled up into his cousins' driveway.

"Oh shit! Big Black, wassup? What the fuck you doin up here?" said one of the cousins. He had like twenty niggas standing around him like he was Scarface and shit.

Black and his cousin walked inside the house.

"Damn, nigga, tell me what's goin on. You good?"

CHAPTER FOURTEEN

DeMarco had to take a trip to New York because LaLa was beefing about how he hadn't seen or spent any time with their newborn daughter Nia, since she was born.

"Guess who's home!" DeMarco called out as he entered the crib.

LaLa looked at him and whispered, "Shhhh! You gonna wake the baby up."

"Come here, girl, show me some love."

"*You* come here," LaLa said with a smile.

"How you and my baby girl been doin?"

"Nigga, please, she in the room. Go and check on her yourself. She looks just like your crazy ass."

DeMarco walked into the bedroom and saw his pretty angel laying in her crib sound asleep. He took her out and laid her onto the bed next to him.

LaLa had that Lil' Kim look and older guys were on her heels. Plus, she showed DeMarco how to do his own thing, so money was nothing to her. Not saying she didn't want the paper, but loyalty was her shit. LaLa had always dreamed of moving out of the projects, but De-Marco didn't want her to. Since he was always running the streets, he didn't want her and the baby at his house by themselves. He figured it was better if she moved back home with her moms.

"Get up, DeMarco, let's go get somethin to eat. I wanna go take family photos at Sears and the baby needs some individual pictures too." LaLa was young, but she was all about family.

They headed out to Green Acres Mall and must have taken at least a hundred pictures. They even bought the small circle picture to go inside a locket. He was so happy to be spending time with LaLa and his baby girl for the first time. DeMarco loved the shit out of his daughter and always wanted to make LaLa happy because he knew without LaLa putting him onto so much shit, he wouldn't be where he was.

"Come on, let's go to Macy's. I saw some stuff I wanna get for the baby."

DeMarco wanted to buy everything he saw for LaLa and his girl.

"DeMarco, ain't that Killer C and some chick in Foot Locker?" LaLa asked.

"Oh shit, girl, you still got that hawk eye!"

They walked over to where the couple was standing, looking at the sneakers on display.

"Nigga, run your shit!" DeMarco said playfully to Killer C. "I could have had your ass."

"Oh shit! What's good, my brotha from another mo-tha? When you got back?"

DeMarco looked at him and smirked. "I told you, I don't kiss and tell."

"Yeah, but wassup, though?"

"Ain't shit, my nigga, just came to get a few things."

"Damn, LaLa, you don't play any games with all those bags. I haven't seen you since DeMarco left."

"Yeah, I'm in the house taking care of my baby."

"Yo, she a keeper, DeMarco. Let me see little Boops. She gettin big, yo. She looks like her daddy."

"You mean just like her motha," LaLa said and rolled her eyes.

Killer C called the salesperson over and asked him if they had Baby Jordans.

"Yes, we do."

"Well, give me two pairs of every Jordan that you have for my goddaughter."

"You mean two pairs of each?"

"Yeah, did I stutter?" he replied.

It took a few minutes for the clerk to gather all the shoes and ring them up. "Okay, that will be $2,100.28."

"Here you go, and keep the change," Killer C said.

"Thank you, sir."

"You welcome. Just remember my face next time."

"No problem, I got you."

"By the way, who this pretty shorty with you?" De-Marco asked.

"Oh, this new joint is Candy, she from Uptown. You know me. I don't do the Queens thing." Killer C always felt like he needed to have something exclusive. Plus, he didn't trust the chicks from Queens or Brooklyn. "I'm sayin, what's your next move DeMarco?"

"I'm gonna spend some quality time with the family, but I'll get at you in the a.m."

"Okay, cool."

DeMarco gave Killer C a pound and they left the store.

DeMarco couldn't wait to get up the next morning so he could go to the BMW dealer to pick up the all-white convertible with the black soft-top and BBS rims he had ordered. He used to love coming back to the hood and stunting on the niggas and bitches who would front on him. DeMarco was the only young nigga in the hood who was getting money like that besides a kid name Boo. Boo had the white-on-white S500 Benz, top-of-the-line shit.

DeMarco pulled up on Killer C and the rest of the niggas who he hadn't seen in a minute, feeling like a million bucks. Chain frozen, wrist frozen, looking like a light show.

"Get in, nigga," DeMarco said to Killer C, and off they went.

They drove through the area with hood eyes on them. DeMarco couldn't believe how his man had the streets on lock. Everywhere they went, Killer C was picking up money.

"Yo, DeMarco, shit changed out here. A lot of niggas fuck with us now. We got this shit in a frenzy. Like those niggas from across town that you didn't like 'cause you was fuckin with that thick shorty you had? Them niggas is buyin bricks from us too."

DeMarco didn't care about any of that. He was a hustler who felt if it made dollars, it made sense.

"Oh yeah, wassup wit my nigga Chief?"

"Oh, he good, DeMarco. He gettin money, you know how that play. When those niggas come out, those punk asses go into hidin. This shit be a ghost town."

"Word!"

They drove out to Killer C's stash house.

"Man, this shit look like a crack house," DeMarco said. "Man, you need to clean this shit up!"

"Nah, I like it like this. Let a nigga run up in here. They would never think they runnin into a gold mine. Check this out, count this." Killer C pulled out the money machine.

They stayed and counted all the money, then split it up.

"I should have another $50,000 for you later on top of that buck."

"Yo, I'm gonna get up with you later," DeMarco said. "We gonna hit the club up tonight. I heard BJ got a spot on Farmers Boulevard. They said all the chicks be there."

"Damn, nigga, you hear everything!"

"Shit, you know I'm in the streets like African feet."

After DeMarco came back from Killer C's stash house, he went by his aunt's to see Money

"Yo, wassup, boy, come outside," he said, after his cousin opened the door.

"Yo, what the fuck?! DeMarco, wassup, stranger?" Money replied.

"Shit, just got back. Damn, I see auntie and them ain't even home. I'ma wait for you out here."

"A'ight, I'll be out in a sec."

DeMarco stayed outside playing with his new Nakamichi system.

Once Money got into the car, the two drove off. De-Marco pulled up to a car wash to leave his vehicle there to get a full detail.

"Yo, Money, hit Killer C's phone and tell him to meet us up here."

"A'ight, cool."

Ten minutes later, Killer C was there with three cars following him.

"Oh shit, where you find this nigga at?"

DeMarco hadn't seen Lefty, a cousin on his father's side, in a few years. Lefty had some lawsuit money, so he had a brand-new BMW wagon.

"This is what the fuck I'm talkin about. Wait till we go out tonight. The bitches is gonna be on us like flies on shit."

"DeMarco, you better not let LaLa catch you." Killer C knew how she was when it came to DeMarco.

"What she doesn't know won't hurt her."

DeMarco and Money jumped in the truck with Killer C and left the car to get detailed.

"Yo, Killer C, get Chief on the phone."

Killer C dialed the number then handed his cell over.

"Yo, boy, wassup, it's DeMarco."

"Wassup, lil' nigga?"

"You, that's wassup. Shit, where you at?"

"Headed to the block."

"A'ight, give me a sec, I'm there."

DeMarco and his crew sat on the block smoking, drinking, and reminiscing on shit they did while growing up. In the hood, you know how it goes. It only takes one person to see you and in less than an hour the block is full of niggas and bitches. DeMarco had so many chicks in the hood they were pulling up like crazy.

"Oh, that's how you do, nigga? You come back in town and don't hit my phone?"

She was a bad little shorty DeMarco had from the northside of Queens. She was dark-skinned with a fat ass; to top it off, she was a twin. "Nah, Keema, I was gonna pop up on you tonight. We goin to J. Boss' club on Farmers. I heard that shit is poppin."

"Yeah, that's what I heard. All I know is you better not have none of these chicks from my side in your face either," she said, with a sassy attitude.

DeMarco smiled, gave her a kiss, and told her he would see her later.

Chief finally pulled up with a few of his shooters

"Yo, what's shakin my nigga? I thought you was never comin back."

"Nah, you know how this game go," DeMarco quickly replied.

From the way DeMarco was looking and talking,

Chief knew DeMarco was now an official boss. De-Marco and Chief stepped to the side and started kicking it. Chief was someone DeMarco looked up to because Chief was a nigga who had the best of both worlds. He was getting money and he had a super gun game.

"But on some real shit, it's good to see you doing your thing," Chief said to DeMarco, feeling proud of him. He'd always seen something in DeMarco, so that just made their relationship better—most real niggas love to see one of their own getting money.

"Yeah, Chief, we going out tonight to J. Boss' spot."

"You know I don't fuck with that club shit, but for you we gonna turn it up. Yeah, and make sure you got them things, DeMarco, because you know how these niggas play."

That's all DeMarco was waiting to hear. He lifted his shirt and pulled out his two seventeen-shot Glocks. "You know I was taught by the best."

DeMarco had moved more money and stepped up his gun game more than Chief realized. His gun game was on Pluto, so New York was a walk in the park.

Money and Lefty slid off to pick up DeMarco's ve-hicle from the car wash. Money pulled back on the block a little while later with a big smile on his face.

"Let me find out that's your joint, DeMarco," Chief said with a grin.

"Yeah, you know I had to keep Southside on the map."

"Hell yeah, especially how young you are with a ma-chine like that. Oh, we gonna have a ball tonight."

"So, Chief, we all gonna meet back up on the block at 11."

"A'ight, cool. I'll get up wit you later," Chief said as he headed to his car and left with his crew following him.

When 11 p.m. rolled around, they must've had twenty cars leaving the block.

"J. Boss, what's good, my nigga?" DeMarco said as he approached the club.

"Ain't shit, boy."

"I see you got the club shit lookin good."

"You already know." J. Boss was another get-money nigga in the hood who DeMarco looked up to. "I'm sayin, how many people you got wit you?"

"To tell you the truth, I have no idea, but check this out, here go $1,500."

"Oh, that's how you doin it?"

"Come on, son, you my nigga. You always gon' be my nigga until the casket drops."

"No doubt."

DeMarco and Chief headed in, and Killer C stepped with them. You had niggas and bitches from all over Queens in the spot. DeMarco noticed a few niggas who he had beef with from back in the day, but he felt at home. He and his crew were at the back of the club, and DJ Grandmaster Vic had the spot jumping. Niggas and bitches from 40 projects, Baisley projects, Merrick Boulevard, Farmers Boulevard, Sutphin Boulevard, Guy Brewer, Henderson, Liberty, and Hollis were all up in there. Bottle after bottle, blunt after blunt, shit was so live niggas were taking turns in the bathroom getting head from chicks. As much as DeMarco loved the ladies, you couldn't pay him to do any shit like that.

"Yo, who that?" DeMarco asked Killer C.

"I don't know, but I know she on you."

The female they were talking about came up to De-Marco and started dancing all over him.

"Who you, shorty?"

"I know you, but you don't know me," she said, in a seductive voice.

"I hear that."

DeMarco thought to himself that whoever she was, she had to be important by the way niggas in the corner were staring at them. This only made him go harder because they were the niggas he'd had beef with back in the day.

Killer C slid up behind DeMarco and whispered in his ear, "Watch yourself. You see them niggas movin funny?"

DeMarco answered Killer C, but never took his eyes off the niggas as he kept dancing with shorty.

"Yo, miss, you gotta name? And who's that, one of your boyfriends over there or somethin?"

"Nah . . . well, he used to be until I spotted you in here," she said, as she grinded up against him even harder.

Killer C whispered in his ear again, "I should go over there and pop one of them niggas."

"My nigga, it's your call," DeMarco replied.

Killer C walked over and put Chief and his niggas on call.

"Yo, shorty, go and get your homegirls and meet us outside," DeMarco said.

The chick smiled and immediately walked off, with her fat ass shaking over to where her girls were standing. DeMarco and his crew exited the club with the girls in tow, and they all hopped in their cars with their women and headed to the block.

"Everybody got a shorty, right?" DeMarco yelled.

Killer C answered with a smile on his face: "You know this, man. I'll see y'all in the a.m."

"Yo, make sure you get at me, DeMarco," Chief said before he jetted off.

As DeMarco pulled up to a light, he noticed two cars following him. He remained calm and didn't say anything to his female friend. He thought his mind was playing tricks on him until he saw another car creeping up slowly.

"Yo, shorty, lay your seat back."

"Anything for you, baby," she replied without a clue as to what was going on.

DeMarco pulled off to the side of the road at the next light. As soon as the other cars pulled up, DeMarco opened fire out the window, letting them niggas have it, like he was James Bond. Shorty was in the passenger seat and pissed on herself, screaming at the top of her lungs. DeMarco wanted to give her a night she would never forget.

He heard two shots coming out the backseat of an all-black Honda Accord. *Okay, this is what these niggas want? I'm gonna give it to them,* he thought to himself.

DeMarco jumped out of the car and stepped into the middle of the street. He got down on one knee, shooting and yelling, "That's what I thought!" Then he hopped back in the car. *I know I hit somebody,* he thought to himself. *Now go tell that.*

Shorty couldn't believe how gangster DeMarco was. She was pissin and damn near cummin in her pants at the same time. "Baby, you a'ight?"

"I'm Gucci," he answered. "This is what we do on the Southside."

"I feel you," she said, in a low voice still a little in shock.

DeMarco jumped on the Van Wyck and headed to the nearest motel. He arrived at the Kew Motor Inn and pulled up into the parking lot.

"Can I help you, sir?" the motel clerk asked.

"Yes, can I please get the jungle room?"

"Sure, that will be $160."

DeMarco handed the lady $200 and told her to keep the change.

"Thank you, sir."

"No problem," he replied.

They headed to the room as he watched her from behind. He couldn't wait to tap that ass. She was still a little overwhelmed from what had just happened, but her desire to fuck DeMarco remained her priority.

"Shorty, before we do anything, let me hold your phone." DeMarco took her phone and removed the battery.

"Can I turn the Jacuzzi on?" she asked.

"Come here. You look like you want to suck on me like a popsicle."

"Damn right I do."

"So what you waiting for?" he asked, releasing his dick from his pants.

She walked over and began sucking so good that De-Marco's eyes rolled to the back of his head.

"Let me stop because you look like you about to bust a nut," she said, with a slight giggle.

"Not until I hit that big fat ass of yours."

"So how you want it, baby?"

"I want that thing from the back," he said.

She lifted her dress and bent over as DeMarco entered her from behind. They fucked for close to an hour in every position possible before they both climaxed. Exhausted, they lay on the bed with the TV on.

"So now you gonna tell me your name or what?"

"My name is China."

"So, where those niggas from?"

China started putting DeMarco onto what type of cars they drove, who they worked for, and where they hung out. DeMarco's phone was once again ringing off the hook and he had already missed fifteen calls. He called Killer C and told him to meet him on the block.

"Damn, nigga, you still got shorty wit you?" Killer C said when he arrived. "That pussy must have been good?"

"I mean on a one-to-ten scale, that shit was a thirty!"

"Word?"

"But check this out, remember those clowns from

last night? They called themselves tryin to run down on the kid at a red light."

"What?"

"But you know me, I lit they asses up like the Fourth of July," DeMarco said.

"Do you know where those niggas from?"

"Yeah, shorty put me on."

"Yeah, she better had," Killer C replied.

"Nah, she good."

"A'ight, I'll send some niggas over there later," Killer C said. He had the right niggas to handle shit like that. "By the way, Skip was saying something about a few of the workers had got robbed."

"Whose workers?"

"I guess y'alls."

"Get Skip on the phone."

Killer C dialed him up.

"Skip, what's the word?"

"Man, you gotta hurry up and get back down here. We didn't make any money in two days."

DeMarco didn't like the sound of that.

"This nigga Black been on some shit, and word is he got his cousin down here from Connecticut. Some nigga named Body," Skip continued to say, with worry in his tone.

"So, how much they took?"

"Man, I don't even wanna tell you, and that's why we haven't worked in two days—me and Bizzy been riding around looking for 'em."

"A'ight, bet, I'm on it." DeMarco hung up the phone.

"Yo, DeMarco, what's good?" Killer C asked anxiously.

"I'll talk to you about it later."

"So where we goin now?"

"I gotta drop shorty off."

The whole ride DeMarco didn't say one word. He was focusing on what he wanted to do to Michelle's brother and his crew. Killer C couldn't wait for him to drop China off, so he could get the scoop.

"Shorty, which way I'm goin?"

"Oh, you can make a left, then a right here by the park; it's the third house from the corner."

He pulled up to her house a minute later.

"So, baby, am I gonna see you tonight?"

DeMarco didn't say a word, he was too wrapped up in his thoughts.

"Just call me. Don't forget."

As soon as she got out, Killer C jumped in the front seat.

"DeMarco, what the fuck happened? Put me on."

"You remember them country niggas I was tellin you about?"

"Yeah, what about them?"

"This nigga Skip talkin about Black and some nigga from Connecticut down there robbin all the workers."

"So what's good?" Killer C asked, with a ready for bloodshed look in his eyes.

"You said you wanted to come down there with me; now is your chance."

"DeMarco, these niggas ain't seen nothin yet. Wait till I touch the town. When we out?"

"First you gotta holla at Money and leave him and Lefty in charge of shit up here. We gotta leave in a couple of days, so make sure everything is taken care of," DeMarco said.

"A'ight, copy."

"You can drop me off by LaLa's mom's crib and take the car."

When they pulled up to LaLa's mom's building, DeMarco looked at Killer C and said, "Don't forget to make sure shit is on point. I don't want no more headaches."

"Okay, I got this, man."

DeMarco got out and walked toward the back of the building. He knew LaLa was going to be tight because he wasn't answering his phone, so he figured he had to give her what she wanted and move her out of the projects.

"So, where you been?" she asked as soon as he walked in.

"I had to make a quick move to Bmore." DeMarco had family down there, so it could have been true—she didn't question it. "Come here, girl. I got a surprise for you."

"What?"

"Nah, I'm dead ass."

"What, boy?"

"I'm movin you and Nia outta the projects."

"When? You told me before I could stay wit you, but that ain't last long."

"I know, but it's gonna be different this time. As soon as you find the place, y'all outta here I promise."

LaLa already knew where she wanted to move. She

was so happy she didn't even stress that DeMarco had been gone for two days.

"So, when could I go look for a house?"

He got up for a minute and came back and passed LaLa $25,000.

"If this isn't enough, let me know and I'll make it happen. Just make sure it's not in the hood."

"Okay, baby," she said as she gave him a big hug and kiss. "Thank you so much!"

"Come on, girl, anything for you and my daughter."

CHAPTER FIFTEEN

DeMarco was ready to leave two days later, but he first wanted to check on Killer C to make sure everything was going according to plan. He pulled up to Killer C's grandmother's house and blew the horn.

"Who is that in front of my house makin noise like they crazy?" yelled the old woman.

"How you doin, Ms. P.?" he said as he rolled down the window.

"I'm doin just fine. How is your grandmother doin?"

"She good."

"Tell her I said hello and you need to talk to your friend. He had two girls in here last night fightin in my house."

"Wow!" DeMarco said.

As Killer C came out of the house shaking his head, his grandmother went back inside.

"You telling me shit got crazy last night?" DeMarco asked, with a smirk on his face.

"Yeah, man, I had shorty from Harlem here and

my BM showed up," Killer C said. "I had to turn into Superman on this bitch. But everything straight. I got shorty outta here!"

"Man, you crazy," DeMarco said with laughter.

"On another note though, all of the BI is taken care of. I gave Money the rundown, and you know he just like you when it comes to gettin that paper. I don't know who's worse," Killer C said, while shaking his head.

"Well, in that case, go get shorty and them from 40, so they can leave in two hours and blend in with the traffic. I don't like leavin too late. You know how the turnpike is," DeMarco replied.

"Word, you right, especially ridin with all that shit." Killer C's beeper went off, interrupting their conversation. "DeMarco, it's 156." The code meant they were ready and they should meet up at their spot.

A half hour later, DeMarco pulled up to the meeting spot in a dark gray Dodge Caravan and Killer C jumped in. Killer C was happy to finally be going with his right-hand man. The two girls DeMarco was bringing along got into their own car and DeMarco followed them.

Both vehicles pulled into the driveway in North Carolina many hours later. DeMarco opened the door and told everybody to go inside, then got into the car the women had been driving and headed down the road. He would never leave work where he rested his head. So he drove over to a nearby farm and hopped out with a big bag, stashing it in his cousin's friend's yard, in a pen full of pigs. He knew nobody would ever go back there because of the way it smelled. When he returned to the house, he pulled both vehicles around the back like nobody was there.

"Damn, DeMarco, this crib is crazy. It look like one of those Long Island joints," Killer C said excitedly.

"I told you, C, I don't play," DeMarco replied, as he powered off his phone.

They all lit up that New York bud and smoked until they couldn't anymore. One by one they fell asleep.

The next morning, DeMarco turned his phone back on. Almost immediately it began to ring.

"Hello?"

"Yo, it's about time you picked up your phone. Boy, I didn't know what happened to you," Michelle said with worry.

"Girl, I'm good."

"I need to see you as soon as possible."

"Okay, cool, where you at?" he responded.

"I'm over at the mall."

"A'ight, meet me in the back of JCPenney. I'll be there in ten minutes."

DeMarco and Killer C pulled up exactly ten minutes later. Michelle started walking toward the car.

"Goddamn, who that?" Killer C asked. "Shorty thick as hell!"

"They say these country girls are the ones to have."

"Oh, I'm gon' have fun down here."

DeMarco sat there quietly watching the parking lot as Michelle jumped into the backseat.

"Wassup, daddy, I missed you." She leaned forward and kissed him on his cheek. "Who is this?"

"My man from up top."

"How are you doing, miss? My name is C."

She smiled.

"Hey, so what's good, Michelle? What's been goin on wit you?"

She started putting him onto what had been happening since he'd left. "Shit's been crazy here. My brother and his crew out here robbin everything movin. Then, this dude from Miami seen me in the club and asked me to give you his number because he need some of your niggas. He said somebody robbed him for some bricks."

"A'ight, cool. Michelle, where your car at?"

"Oh, it's on the other side of the mall."

"Hit my phone later, girl, and we gon' get up."

"A'ight, daddy." She gave him another kiss and they pulled off.

"Damn, son, you got it like that down here?"

"I wouldn't trade this for nothin else."

"Word, so wassup with these niggas Skip and Bizzy?"

"Oh, we gonna check them niggas right now."

A few minutes later, they pulled up. DeMarco rolled down his window.

"Oh shit, you playin, my nigga! We thought y'all was the boys," Bizzy said.

"Oh shit! Bizzy, come here!" DeMarco shouted from the car.

"Yo, look, he got this nigga Killer C with him." Skip got up off the step and walked to the car.

"Oh yeah, it's on now for real. C, what up!" Bizzy said as he came outside.

"You already know, my nigga."

"So what are we gonna do about this nigga Black and his crew? Them niggas been layin low, because me and Bizzy would've been on them."

DeMarco sat there with his hands crossed, piecing the plot together in his mind. He liked to think about every possible angle before putting a plan into action.

When they got inside the crib, they couldn't believe their eyes. The room was full of guns and bags with money.

"Oh, this is what I'm takin 'bout," Killer C said, holding out an AK-47 and an M16. "Oh, watch what I do to these niggas."

DeMarco looked at all the money that Skip and Bizzy had made, still thinking of their next move.

"Listen, we gonna get these niggas on my time, but right now we gonna get this money. All we gotta do is beef up security for now. When niggas out there hustlin, have one pitchin, while you got the other two with straps on them. And get the whole crew walkie-talkies and scanners and everybody wear all black. I'ma show y'all how to make this real money."

"But niggas might think we soft because we let them niggas run off with all that money."

"Let me tell you somethin, Skip, that's why you stay in jail all the time—'cause you don't think first. Money is power and power is respect, you got that?"

"I got you. A'ight, let's do this."

Skip and Bizzy headed to RadioShack.

* * *

"Yo, Skip, we gotta make sure this works, 'cause we could cut DeMarco's man out. We could've been in New York going through all type of shit, and instead he got us livin good."

Bizzy wasn't trying to go back to New York anytime soon, so they did everything according to plan. Shit was moving like clockwork and just that quickly they had their spot set up. Word started traveling all over the town. DeMarco's crew was nothing to fuck with; they spread that message loud and clear. His structure and his security were so tight that niggas just got scared and started speeding off.

"Yo, DeMarco, does Michelle have any bad-ass friends that look like her?" Killer C asked.

"Oh shit, I'm glad you said somethin because I almost forgot to get up with them. Pass me your phone, let me call her real quick."

After the third ring she picked up. "Who this?"

"It's me, DeMarco."

"Oh hey, daddy, wassup?"

"I want you and your girls to meet me in the Golden Corral parking lot."

"Okay, we on our way there."

Ten minutes later, she pulled up in the parking lot and rolled down her window. Before anyone got out of the car, DeMarco told them to follow him. He hopped right on the highway to I-95 south.

* * *

Beep beep beep!

"Oh shit! I'm thinking that's DeMarco out there," Rah said aloud with a big smile on his face.

"Man, how you know that's him?" Jazz replied.

"Nigga, you sleep too hard. You didn't hear the three beeps?"

They both went to the front door. "Yo, DeMarco, y'all pull around the back of the house."

"I hope you got that good-smelling stuff."

"You know I don't leave home without it. Here, fill up a few blunts." Rah passed everybody their own.

Killer C didn't smoke, so he was looking for a drink. "Y'all don't have no liquor in here?"

"Yeah, we do," Jazz said and went into the house. He came back outside a moment later with two bottles of Jack Daniel's.

"Damn, you tryna kill a nigga," Killer C said and began to laugh.

"We heard a lot about you and how you get down," Jazz said.

"Man, I'm good. Just came out here to hold my nigga down, that's all."

Tia and Kee-Kee were looking at Killer C like fresh meat.

"Yo, DeMarco, let's go into the house. Jazz and me got somethin to show you," Rah said.

Inside, DeMarco's eye got wide looking at all the money—ten bricks stacked up damn near the ceiling.

"Yo, Rah, go tell my man C to come here." DeMarco was sure he could trust Killer C with just about anything.

A few seconds later, Rah walked back into the room with Killer C a couple steps behind him.

"What the fuck is this?" Killer C asked with a curious smile on his face.

"Remember when shorty was in the car talking about them niggas got robbed for some bricks?" DeMarco said.

"How we gonna move all this money?" Killer C asked.

"Shit, if there's a will, there's a way," DeMarco replied. He had family all over the South, and to top it all off, his uncle owned a funeral home. So as far as he was concerned, he could come get that money and put it inside one of those caskets.

DeMarco slid off like he was going to the bathroom and called his uncle. He told him what he wanted to do and how to get to the house. Then he swapped the house keys off Jazz's ring.

Then, with excitement in his voice, he said "Check this out we all goin down to my favorite spot, Myrtle Beach."

They all jumped into their cars and headed out.

When they arrived, they rented two rooms connected to each other.

"Y'all know wassup," Michelle said to her two homegirls as they walked into the shower together.

"Yo, DeMarco, I can't lie, this is the life, my nigga," Killer C said with a Kool-Aid smile. "Man, New York chicks don't move like that. You got to fight to get the pussy. I see why once you come down here you take forever to come back to NY."

DeMarco started rolling up some blunts.

"Which one you gonna let me get?"

"Nigga, Michelle is off limits. That's my boo right there."

Kee-Kee and Tia came out of the shower butt naked. Killer C couldn't believe how these country chicks worked in the South.

DeMarco walked into the bathroom with Michelle and they both got into the shower. Michelle felt so special and thought to herself, *I'd never turn my back on this nigga for nobody, not even my punk-ass ol' brother.*

DeMarco started fucking the shit out of her in the shower, all over the sink, against the wall, everywhere, you name it.

She whispered in his ear, "Daddy, you gotta go out there and fuck these bitches. You know what I'm sayin? So we can keep them on the team."

On the real tip, Michelle was a real bitch. They went out into the room to find the others waiting.

"Y'all took forever," Kee-Kee said, thirsty for some dick.

Killer C was already underneath the covers waiting to tear one of them up. Michelle looked at Kee-Kee and gave her the nod. She jumped on DeMarco like a dog in heat. Kee-Kee and Tia switched between DeMarco and Killer C as Michelle sat and watched. Killer C was in heaven.

DeMarco's phone rang, interrupting their small orgy. He got up and walked to the bathroom. It was his uncle.

"What's good?"

"Okay, I'm here, where did you say the key was at?"

"Under the front rug," said DeMarco.

"Hold on a minute." He returned to the phone a few seconds later. "A'ight, boy, I see you when I see you, like always."

"Okay, cool, unc."

When DeMarco walked back out of the bathroom, it looked like a movie set. One thing was for certain: country girls loved New York niggas!

"Yo, what's that noise?" DeMarco asked.

They heard somebody moaning in the next room. DeMarco walked to the attached door, peeked inside, and saw his cousins with four chicks getting their porn on. He smiled and closed the door.

"What was it?" Killer C asked.

"That's them niggas over there with a few chicks."

"Where they get 'em from?" Killer C wanted a piece of the action.

"Last time we was down here, them niggas was in a strip club makin it rain, so they must've hooked back up with them."

"Word? Oh a'ight. I'm sayin, where is the ice machine? I'm thirsty as hell."

"Oh, you gotta go to the long hallway. It's right next to the Pepsi machine," DeMarco replied.

Killer C hopped up and walked out. DeMarco already knew what he was really up to: he was sliding next door to get a piece of that action.

"Here, daddy," Tia said and passed DeMarco the blunt.

Michelle went to put the chain on the door and gave Kee-Kee a devilish grin. "Now we are *really* gonna play doctor," she said.

They started going in on one another. Tia was licking the shit out of Michelle's pussy while Kee-Kee had De-Marco's dick in her mouth. DeMarco loved every minute of it.

"I'm saying wassup, are we gonna stay in the hotel all day, daddy?" Michelle asked.

"Nah, let's get dressed and hit the club tonight. They have a lot of good spots down here," DeMarco replied, then went to take a shower while Michelle schooled her girls.

"Listen, when we get to the club, try to get every number of any nigga that look like a baller. We tryna have daddy rob everything movin. You see last time he bought damn near the whole mall for us. This time he gon' buy all of us cars."

DeMarco and his crew went to the club on the beach and bought out the whole VIP section. They even had niggas and chicks they didn't know in their section. The girls were doing their thing. Baller after baller, Kee-Kee had so many numbers in her phone that she had to borrow Michelle's phone to add more.

CHAPTER SIXTEEN

"All rise for the Honorable Judge Steven Goldberg." DeMarco stood next to his lawyer wearing a black suit and tie.

The bailiff began speaking: "Jones docket #95J2826, *The People vs. DeMarco Jones,* assault with a deadly weapon, possession of a firearm, and attempted murder in the second degree."

"How do you plead, Mr. Jones?"

DeMarco's lawyer, Mr. Walter Vanzetta, said, "Not guilty."

"Does the state have anything to say?" the judge asked.

"Yes we do, Your Honor. We need more time to investigate this case," the prosecutor replied.

"Okay, the next court date will be August 12th."

DeMarco and Mr. Vanzetta left the courtroom.

"Mr. Vanzetta, what you think the outcome will be?" DeMarco asked as he passed him $5,000, all in hundreds.

"Mr. Jones, I'm confident we will beat this. If you ask me, it's a self-defense case. I just have to prove you were trying to protect yourself from being attacked."

DeMarco was confident in his attorney and felt at ease as they parted. His next stop was to check in with his bail bondsman to mark his court appearance and take note of the next court date. When he arrived, there was a lady at the front desk who he hadn't seen before.

"May I help you, sir?"

"Yes, my name is DeMarco Jones. I had to go to court today, and my next court date is August 12th."

"Okay, give me one minute, sir." She walked off to the back of the office.

DeMarco sat there patiently waiting for her to return.

"Excuse me, sir. We have you marked down, so everything is clear."

"Okay, thanks a lot. Oh, can you tell me what happened to the other people that used to work here?" He was trying to avoid saying any names.

"They still work here. You know India? Her boyfriend and her had to go out of town to catch a few people. You know when you youngsters get rabbit and everyone runs away."

DeMarco didn't even reply. He nodded his head and walked out with a smile on his face. On his way to the car, he couldn't believe what he was seeing. *Oh, I know that ain't that nigga Black.*

The dude looked over at him with an evil stare and pulled up to DeMarco's car just as DeMarco was getting into it.

"Yo, what up, city slicker?"

"You tell me, country bumpkin," DeMarco replied.

"Yeah, okay, New York boy," he spat.

Black and his homeboy immediately drove off. Little did they know DeMarco was clutching the six-shot .357 that he kept in his stash box. DeMarco pulled his fitted Yankee cap down and played track three off the Nas *Illmatic* CD: "Life's a Bitch."

When DeMarco got back to the house, Killer C was out like a light. DeMarco stared at his phone wondering what his next move was. He noticed that he had two missed calls from Michelle, so he called her back.

"Wassup, girl?"

"Ain't shit. That big-eye boy from Miami gave me a number and told me to have you call him. I don't know what he's really talkin about, but he thirsty."

"A'ight, cool. I'll hit you back in a minute."

"A'ight."

DeMarco immediately dialed the number. After the third ring, the kid picked up.

"Who dis?"

"This is DeMarco."

"Oh, man, this is Gee. I been trying to get up wit you, my nigga."

"So what's good? What's the word?"

"Listen, my nigga, can you meet me at your cousin's house?"

"What cousin?" asked DeMarco.

"Colg. That's my boy right there, my nigga."

"A'ight, I'm on my way."

DeMarco then called Colg. "Yo, wassup, it's DeMarco."

"Ain't shit. Wassup with y'all?"

"I was callin to ask you wassup wit the nigga Gee."

"That's good people right there. He's been tryin to get up with you for a minute. You know that nigga Black that you shot? Word is that him and his crew took ten birds from them."

"Word?" DeMarco was shocked.

"Yeah, so he wanted you and him to lock the whole town down together."

"Well, I'm on my way out to your house to see wassup."

"A'ight, cuz, I'm waitin on you."

Colg knew that DeMarco didn't play, so he wanted to make sure everything went smoothly; plus, he could make a lot of money if things turned out right.

"C, get up!" DeMarco yelled.

"Wassup, DeMarco? Damn, what time is it?"

"Man, it's that time, 2:30."

C hopped up and lit his blunt as DeMarco put the plan together in his mind. DeMarco started putting him onto what this kid Gee was saying.

"A'ight, DeMarco, let's strap up and go over there."

DeMarco stopped on the side of the road and told Killer C to walk down to Colg's house through the woods in the back.

"DeMarco, if this nigga ain't by himself, we gon' let him have it. If I take my hat off, you know what it's hittin for."

"A'ight, let's dance."

DeMarco pulled up to Colg's house with all of his windows down—he wanted to make sure he could get a clean shot if needed. Colg and Gee came out of the crib smoother than the Fonz.

"Yo, wassup, my nigga?"

"Same ol' shit, tryna make a dollar outta fifteen cents."

"I hear you, my nigga, but I heard this nigga Black took some shit from you."

"Yeah, some light shit."

"I'm gonna keep it solid wit you, my nigga. Them niggas was so thirsty I had another ten joints in the crib."

DeMarco's mouth dropped thinkin to himself, *This stupid bitch!* That's when his mind clicked. If these niggas got caught for ten, and still had ten, but weren't too worried about the loss, imagine what they really had.

"So I'm saying, Gee, what you tryna do?"

"Man, I'm tryna wipe them niggas out."

DeMarco started laying down the game plan. Gee couldn't believe how swift he was for a young guy; he loved every word of it.

"So, DeMarco, check this out. I'm gonna give you ten birds. Just bring me back $18,000 and $5,000 for your cuz, which is a total of $23,000. I want to make sure my nigga Colg get his cut."

"Okay, $18,000, and $5,000 for Colg. Be back here tonight. We will have that for you, Gee. Just sit back and watch how your money grow," DeMarco said with a smile.

That's all Gee wanted to hear. DeMarco's team was strong throughout that area. "A'ight, I gotta make a run," he said, then hopped on his motorcycle and sped off.

Killer C came out of the woods. "I hope that shit was worth it, because them bugs tore my ass up," he said.

Colg stood there wondering what DeMarco was up to. "I told you, DeMarco, that boy Gee is the man. He just don't have no family down here. His brother is in the military, so that's how he heard of this town getting all this money."

"So, Colg, where you meet him at?"

"I met him at the bike show."

"Oh, okay," DeMarco said. It was starting to make sense. The more Colg talked, the more DeMarco started putting things together.

DeMarco and Killer C jumped back in the car and DeMarco called out the window to Colg, "Holla at me later." After a few minutes on the road, he smiled and said, "Yo, C, I could never forget one thing my pops used to say to me before he went to jail. He used to be like, *Listen, boy, you need to do more and say less or you'll be shopping at Payless.*"

"What he meant by that?"

"He was basically sayin that actions speak louder than words."

"Oh, I get you!"

"Do you know what just happened?" DeMarco said. "That's the same nigga that we just caught for ten joints. He thinks it was that nigga Black and his crew that did it."

"Word?"

"Well, he's givin us ten more tonight. So now that's doin more and sayin less."

DeMarco showed Killer C that day that he was one of the best to ever do it. They got to the crib and De-Marco went into his room. He closed his door and pulled his Bible out before dropping to his knees and praying. See, one thing about DeMarco is that he always believed in God and was very spiritually oriented. He knew at this point that all of his blessings were coming through. He could remember a time when he was driving on the highway with a few birds in the car and a state trooper started following him and his cousin Swimmy. The two of them started making calls to his older sister who was heavy into church. They asked her to start praying for them, then, out of nowhere, the state trooper made a U-turn on the highway and went the opposite way. There were so many reasons why he always loved God.

Knock knock.

"Yo! DeMarco, what's good?" Killer C had something to tell his right-hand man.

"I'm coming out now," DeMarco said, then put his Bible in the top drawer and opened the door. "Wassup, son?"

"You know what, DeMarco? You my nigga for real. I mean, I was gettin money in New York, but look what we had to do to get it. You bring me down here and this shit fall right in your lap." Killer C had always thought he needed to be violent when it came to getting money, but DeMarco saw it a whole different way.

"C, you already know how we do. My Uncle Bruh damn near raised both of us, so it's only right for us to get this money together."

They just chilled out and smoked until 8 o'clock came. DeMarco looked at his phone and saw that Colg had been trying to reach him since 7, so he called him back.

"What's good, Colg?"

"Man, you need to come pick your clothes up."

That was all DeMarco needed to hear. DeMarco and C got there in record time. They started loading bricks up in the back of Colg's truck.

"Yo, Colg, I'm gonna need your truck for a minute."

"Go ahead, be my guest."

All Colg had was money on his mind. He knew once DeMarco got the bricks in his hands, it was going to be no looking back. DeMarco and C ran into the woods and stashed the bricks one by one, and then pulled back up to Colg's house. DeMarco backed up his own car, then hit his brakes a few times before opening his stash box.

"Yo, Colg, here's the first down payment." DeMarco threw his cousin $25,000. Colg's eyes got as big as a truck tire. "Come on, Colg, if it wasn't for you this would've never happened. Just remember, family comes first."

"A'ight, bo, I'm witcha."

They pulled out of Colg's driveway and headed into town to check on Skip and Bizzy.

Bizzy and Skip had shit jumping.

"Yo, Skip, there go DeMarco and C."

"Yo, wassup, nigga?"

"Damn, Skip, this shit looking crazy. I mean, it's niggas and bitches everywhere."

"The funny thing is, DeMarco, we hustle two blocks down. This is just where everybody hangs at. Anyway, I been wantin to talk to you."

"What's good?"

"Nah, I got some people in the next town over that be buyin joints."

"Where you meet them at?"

"Me and Bizzy be takin the team to the mall there, so I bagged a nice redbone chick with a fat ass. I been seein her for a minute. Matter of fact, she's pregnant."

"Oh, here we go," DeMarco said with a sigh.

"Nah, for real, DeMarco, she good peoples. But her brothers and cousins do their thing."

"A'ight, so what you told them?"

"You can get it for $46,000 a joint."

"Shit, Skip, you might as well tell them you can get that fire for $47,500, so you can make you a lil' profit," DeMarco said. "So this is what I'm gonna do. I'm gonna let you and C handle that. When you want it, call him. He got you. Just make sure you always by yourself."

"Come on, nigga, we from up top and Rakim said it the best: *No mistakes allowed.*"

"Okay, I gotta go bust a move real quick. Yo, C, you good?"

"I'm great."

"You sure?"

"Yeah, why, wassup? You can leave me out here with Skip and Bizzy till later."

"Y'all niggas better not start no shit," DeMarco said. "Nah, we good."

DeMarco knew what C was up to. See, Killer C wanted to get out there, see how shit was moving, and try to bag him one of those country girls so he could start spreading his wings. Look how his man Skip met a girl in the mall and her brother and cousins were now buying bricks. That's all he needed if niggas were trustworthy. C stood out there and saw his men from NY have shit moving like New Jack City. He couldn't wait to get his chance.

Skip looked at C and said, "Wait until we go to the pool hall tonight. All the bad chicks be up in that spot."

CHAPTER SEVENTEEN

It was the first night Killer C went out without DeMarco. He wanted to see what the town was made of. At the pool hall, he went to the bar and ordered three Long Island Iced Teas. The spot started getting packed as the night went on. He just sat at the bar scoping out the place. Skip and Bizzy had chicks all over them. Around 10 p.m., Skip walked up to C with a fine brown-skinned chick with a little mole on the top of her lip and a fat ass.

"Yo, Killer C, this homegirl Dana."

"Oh, how are you doin?" she asked Killer C with a strong country accent. "You want a few drinks with me?"

"I don't mind, but first thing before we chill . . . do you have a baby father or a man in here?"

"No, I don't. The guy I used to mess with is locked up; he got ten years for shooting somebody."

"When does he come home? If you don't mind me askin."

"Nah, I don't, but I can tell you one thing: no time soon."

The lady behind the bar asked them if they needed anything. She smiled, knowing C wasn't from around there.

"Yes ma'am, can I have a straw, please?" Dana said.

"What about you, young man?"

"I'll take another Long Island Iced Tea with no ice."

Killer C was feeling good. Before long, he and shorty were drunk. Dana was feeling his style, and he was feeling her.

"So, what else you do?"

"Oh, I go to school and I work. What about you?"

He paused, then said the first thing that came to his mind: "I'm a pharmacist. So, what are you doin later tonight?"

"Not much. I'll probably go home to bed." Dana pulled her chair closer to C.

At that moment, Skip walked back up with two more girls. "See, I told you that you'd like my man, Dana."

"I ain't gonna lie, Skip, he is the sweetest. The girls in the South already know them boys from New York get that real money. Especially DeMarco's crew."

"Damn, shorty, this little pool hall is like a club," Killer C observed.

"Hell yeah, this is where everybody at on Wednesdays and Thursdays."

"So, Dana, you live by yourself?"

"I sure do. I'm an independent woman. I work for my shit."

"I hear that. So where is the place at, independent woman?"

"Not too far from here. I live right behind the police station," Dana replied.

Killer C knew a nigga wasn't crazy enough to run up in there.

"I'm getting tired, Killer."

"It's Killer C, but you can call me C."

"Okay, C, here's my number if you want to get up later or somethin."

After Dana split, Killer C ordered one more drink and headed over to Skip at the pool table. The nigga Bizzy was in the corner getting head from some tall-ass chick. *I thought country niggas be on some shit with niggas from New York,* C said to himself.

"What you think, my nigga?"

"Shit, Skip, y'all got this shit on lock."

"Your boy DeMarco paved the way for us down here. Yo, C, I'm saying, what y'all niggas doin tonight?"

"Man, all you gotta do is get me a pistol and drop me off at shorty's house."

Skip knew Dana was good money, so he didn't mind his man going over there. Shit, even he had tried to get with Dana, but she wouldn't give him none.

While everybody was partying and dancing, Skip and Killer C slid out. When they pulled up to Dana's driveway, Skip passed C a seventeen-shot Glock.

"Yo, what the fuck is this, Skip?"

"Nigga, you in the South, they got all types of shit down here."

"You ain't never lied, my nigga. I ain't never seen no shit like this in New York."

Killer C pulled his phone out and called Dana. She answered on the first ring like she was waiting for him to call or something.

"Hello," she said in her sexiest voice.

"Hey, I'm outside."

"Okay, I'm coming to the door now."

"I'll see you in the a.m.," C said to Skip.

"No doubt. You got the number—if anything comes up, hit my phone."

"Copy."

C walked up the stairs but couldn't see very well because the porch lights were off. When he opened the door, he found Dana butt-ass naked. C just stood there with his eyes wide open.

"What you gonna do, stay there or close the door? What, you ain't never seen nobody naked before?"

"I ain't hardly sayin that."

"So what are you sayin then?"

C looked at her and smiled, then followed her inside the house. "Shorty, can I light a blunt in here?"

"I mean, C, what you think, I'm a nun? Light that thing up and pass me some."

C was feeling everything about Dana. They fucked all night and by the morning C felt like he'd been with her for years. She gave him the keys to her house, car, and had him drop her off at work.

C couldn't wait to see DeMarco to show him how fast he made moves.

* * *

"Yo, who the fuck is that?" DeMarco jumped out of bed and grabbed India's gun. "Stay here, I be right back."

DeMarco opened the house door. "Yo, C who the fuck car is that?"

"You know me, DeMarco, I make moves."

"Okay, make moves. But whose shit is that?"

"Oh, this chick named Dana I bagged at the pool hall last night."

"You talkin about shorty that live downtown?"

"Yeah, that's her."

"Oh, she's a keeper. She wouldn't even give *me* that pussy!"

"That's crazy. Skip told me the same shit. I thought he was frontin."

"Nah, she good, we need her on this team."

"Daddy, are you a'ight?" India appeared in the hall.

"Didn't I tell you to stay in the room?"

"Boy, you not my father. I'm old enough to be your mother, and bring my gun back in here before you do somethin stupid!"

"Yo, DeMarco, who the fuck is that, my nigga? She is super bad. She looks like an Indian."

"That's my bail bondsman joint."

"Man, you fucking the bail bondsman chick too? Oh, high five, you the man. Yo, DeMarco, I gotta take a nap here. I was up all night with shorty and I don't have to pick her up until 5 anyway."

"Okay, cool, but make sure you park that car in the back of the house."

"Got you."

DeMarco headed back to the bedroom to get some of that ol' donkey.

CHAPTER EIGHTEEN

DeMarco left Killer C in the house sound asleep while he and India went over to his grandmother's place to check on his sisters and brothers.

"Long time no see, Big Man." That was a nickname his grandmother had called him ever since he was a baby. She said she always knew DeMarco was going to be the man.

"Hi, Grandma, how you been?"

"I'm fine, boy, are you hungry?" She always tried to feed him whenever he came over. "How are you, India?"

"I'm okay, Mrs. Jones."

DeMarco walked into each of his sisters' and brothers' rooms and gave them $2,000 apiece. They were so happy. He had three sisters and two brothers, along with a few half-brothers on his father's side. They just followed him all over the house like he was the president or something.

When DeMarco felt himself moving too fast, he'd go

over to his grandmother's house and sit by the fireplace where she kept a picture of his mother next to her ashes.

He sat there talking with his grandfather and sipped on the old man's favorite drink, Gordon's Gin. His grandpa loved that light liquor. DeMarco used to get twisted quick when he drank it because it was too strong for him.

His grandmother and India sat on the porch for at least an hour. The two women were very close. Grandma had a special love for India because she knew she would always be there for her grandson.

DeMarco was soon ready to get up out of there, but before he and India left he told her to get the black bag from the car. When she brought it to him, he motioned his head to tell her to give it to his grandmother. When his grandma opened it, she started to cry. She had never seen so many hundred-dollar bills in her life.

"DeMarco," she said, "what am I supposed to do with this?"

"Do what you want with it, Grandma. I love you. I'll see you later. I got a few more runs to make and I'll be back soon."

When DeMarco got back to the crib, Killer C was gone.

"Where'd he go?" India asked.

"He must've left to pick shorty up from work."

India gave him that look and pushed him into the bedroom and down onto the bed. She pulled his dick out of his pants and went to work. She was an older chick, but she loved having sex and DeMarço never stopped her. India was his ace in the hole; he gave her whatever she wanted. He even gave her $100,000 up front just in case one of his homeboys ever got into trouble. She liked that about him—out of all the young dudes she'd dealt with, he was always about his business.

"Girl, chill, that's that nigga coming in." India got off his dick a little mad because she didn't get her shit off.

DeMarco walked to the front door. "Yo, C, I thought you went to pick shorty up from work."

"Nah, not till 5," he said. C had two big Reebok bags in his hands. "Check this out. Me and Skip just made a quick move with that kid who said he wanted to buy that joint. Well, they bought five of them things. Them niggas get paper and they wasn't on no funny shit because he was by himself and all the money wasn't in hundred-dollar bills. You can tell it was straight block money."

"So where Skip at?" DeMarco asked.

"He took his shorty to the doctor. You know she really pregnant."

DeMarco told India to come out of the bedroom. "Baby, I need you to take this money and put it up."

They counted all the money, then India left.

"Yo, C, I want to get this dude Gee his money by Friday, so we can cop some more joints. So after you get shorty from work, go check Skip and Bizzy and see what they workin with."

"Cool, I got you, bro," Killer C said.

"But don't let them know about Gee."

"Don't even worry about that, I got you."

It was time for DeMarco to do some homework, so he called up Tia. "Yo, where you at?"

"I'm over here at the She Thing hair salon. I'll be done in about fifteen minutes."

"A'ight, cool, just meet me at the Dash Inn."

"Okay."

DeMarco had been fucking Tia on the low without Kee-Kee and Michelle. After hanging up the phone, he decided to go pick her up directly from the salon. She jumped in the car as soon as he arrived. He had her take him to every last stash house Black and his crew had. DeMarco wanted to make sure nobody on the street had any product but him and his crew. He had some cousins from the area who were good at running up in houses. Tia would tell him anything and do anything for him. Since she obviously wanted to take Michelle's spot, De-Marco pulled his Nike sweatpants down and Tia started giving him head. She always acted like she was a porn star.

DeMarco didn't even tell her he was about to let go; he just came in her mouth and all over her face and hair.

"Damn, boy," she yelled, "you know I just got my hair done!"

"My bad, I couldn't help it." DeMarco passed her his T-shirt, $1,000, and then he dropped her back at the salon.

"Look, boy, is any of that stuff in my hair?"

"No, you good, babe. Hit me later."

DeMarco went straight to his cousins' house and gave

them the rundown. By the end of the night, them niggas had wiped out all of Black's spots.

"Here, y'all take this $20,000 and lay low for a week or so, but keep y'all ears to the streets."

"No doubt, cuz, you already know I'm on point."

DeMarco's cousins knew that whenever he called them, there was money involved.

Later on, his phone rang, "Yo, wassup, daddy?" Michelle asked.

"Nothin, just chillin," DeMarco answered. "What's good wit you?"

Michelle explained how the niggas from Miami had robbed all of her punk-ass brother's spots, taking everything, TVs and all. They even killed his dogs.

"So what are they gonna do about it?" DeMarco asked.

"I guess him and my cousin Body riding around lookin for them niggas."

Everything was going exactly as planned. Now, all the money would come to him. They thought it was the Miami boys, the Miami boys would think it was them, and now Gee was going to put a price on their heads.

Three days went by, and DeMarco was laying low, putting the rest of his plot together before hitting up Colg and Gee for the bricks.

"A'ight, DeMarco, I'm gon' get on that now," Colg said, then delivered his cousin's message. Two hours later, Gee was there at Colg's crib. This time DeMarco was by himself, but he knew Gee wasn't going to try any bullshit.

"I can't lie to you, DeMarco, you my kind of nigga," Gee said with a big smile on his face.

DeMarco gave Gee the duffel bag and they counted the money. Every dollar was well on point.

DeMarco started putting Gee onto the word on the streets. Gee couldn't believe what he was hearing. He wasn't a tough guy, but he had plenty of money and would do whatever it took to get even.

"Oh, word? These fuck boys wanna fuck wit me?"

"My nigga, I'm gonna show them how we play back home."

Gee was hot as fire. "Listen, DeMarco, I got twenty of them things for you in the house, but I have a better idea. Give me the same number on fifteen of the things, and the other five . . . keep those. Just make sure you get somebody to handle them boys."

"Don't worry, Gee, I got this under control. Like I told you before, just chill and put your feet up."

DeMarco jumped in Colg's truck and headed to the woods. DeMarco ran into the trees in a flash to stash the bricks before anybody could see him, then drove back to Colg's house and called him outside.

"Yo, Colg, what are you doing with all your money?"

"Man, I'm just living and shit. If it wasn't for you, I wouldn't be doing nothin. All the chicks love me."

DeMarco was just shooting the shit to see where his cousin's head was. He wanted to make sure everybody was still on the same page.

"Yo, cuz, I'm gonna keep it real, my nigga. Gee must like you."

"Why you say that?" DeMarco asked.

"Why I say that? Because he told me if everything go right with this clown Black, he would give you five more. He got a coke factory. He gotta have a connect that get it straight from the Mexican border."

"That's all I needed to hear." DeMarco's mind started racing.

He hung up with Colg, and glanced down at his phone: *Damn, who left all these messages?* He dialed the number. After the second ring, Skip picked up.

"Yo, what's good, Skip?"

"I know you comin out wit me tonight? You forgot it's my birthday?" Skip yelled through the phone.

"Oh shit, with all this runnin around, I almost forgot. Where you want to go?" DeMarco asked.

"I'm tryna do Planet Rock tonight."

"A'ight, bet, we there."

DeMarco drove two hours away to pick up his cousins Jazz and Rah and they all headed to the mall.

"What you trying to get, DeMarco?"

"You know me, I'm a Queens dude. I'm gonna get the all-black Adidas pants with the stripes and some black-shell toes."

"I'm with you," Rah said.

Jazz was a different type of nigga, so he rocked his own style. That's just how he was.

* * *

Planet Rock's parking lot was looking like Summer Jam. There were people all over the place, from everywhere. DeMarco skipped the whole line and walked up to his man Big Dimp who was the bouncer and slid him five 100-dollar bills. He took DeMarco and his cousins right in and didn't even search them.

Big Dimp pointed to the VIP section and said, "Yo, DeMarco, there go your people right over there."

Skip, C, and Bizzy were there with all their niggas and some chicks.

"Yo, DeMarco, wassup, nigga?"

"Ain't shit. Damn, C, I thought you was lost."

"Me? Nah, a nigga been out here makin it do what it do."

"Wassup wit homegirl?"

"Oh, she good. She up in here somewhere."

"Let's go see wassup wit the birthday boy." DeMarco loved his niggas. "Yo, Skip, happy birthday!" He went into his pocket and passed his man an all-gold Rolex with a diamond face.

"Yo, good fuckin lookin, my nigga. Word." Skip knew he was certified in DeMarco's book.

The more DeMarco looked around, the more bitches he saw there who he had fucked. Even Michelle was up in there with her crew. They just acted as if they didn't know each other in public.

Everybody started to come up to DeMarco like it was *his* birthday. Bizzy just laid in the cut in case a nigga tried to front, which was the last thing on DeMarco's mind because he was strapped up.

They popped bottles, tossed bottles, smoked blunts, you name it. His team was having fun and the DJ was giving shout-outs to DeMarco and his crew all night. "Big up to DeMarco and the get-money get-bitches crew!"

At some point DeMarco noticed a bouncer holding somebody back from getting in the VIP area. He asked his man Cash, "Do you know them dudes?"

"Yeah, that's Black's cousin Body."

"Oh, word? Tell the bouncer to let them niggas up in here."

DeMarco was a getting-money nigga, but he wasn't afraid of anything. The bouncer moved out of the way and let them in.

Killer C appeared out of nowhere. "Wassup? May I help you? This is a private party." DeMarco's whole crew pulled out pistols.

"Nah, it's not like that, yo. I just wanna holla at your man. Ain't no beef or anything like that."

"I know it ain't," Killer C said with an ice grill. "You can come up, but your boys gotta stay outside of VIP."

"No problem, cuz," Body said, and walked up to De-Marco. "Wassup, I heard a lot about you."

"Ain't shit. Now get to the point."

"DeMarco, I am feeling your style. I heard from a few dudes and chicks that you a good guy and you take care of your crew. See, my grimy-ass cousin came and got me from my Connecticut. He told me a different story about how you and your people ran in his crib, robbed, and shot him and his homeboy Man-Man. Then I came to find out it was the opposite way around and the bitch-ass snitched on you! I don't fuck wit snitches at all."

DeMarco just listened and didn't say a word.

"But on some real shit, DeMarco, I'm tryna get money with y'all. My nigga cousin is a cold snake. He brought us all the way down here for bullshit. I had to meet a chick who works in the mall, so me and my dudes would have somewhere to stay. To top it all off, she put me onto some Ohio cat with $300,000 in the crib. I sent Black in there to get it and he only came out with $50,000."

DeMarco looked Body in his eye and asked him, "How do you know it was $300,000?"

"Quiet as kept, shorty was fuckin one of the niggas and she took a picture of it and showed it to me."

Body was drunk, but it seemed to DeMarco like he was telling the truth.

"I'm saying, DeMarco, we all from up north. It's only right we get this money. I'm on the run from CT, so I don't got nothin to lose. I gotta get it!"

Now DeMarco was sure it wasn't a setup because nobody would tell his business like that.

"Okay, we gon' see you around. What's your number? I'll have somebody holla at you."

Michelle was watching her cousin talk to DeMarco. She just wanted things to work out with her cousin and Black, but she didn't realize her cousin wasn't messing with Black and Man-Man anymore.

DeMarco told Cash to give Body a bottle of Moët and Body walked back into the party.

Killer C wanted to put his whole clip in Body and

his two homeboys. "Yo, DeMarco, what that nigga talkin about?"

"I'll tell you later, but one thing is for certain: we got us one," DeMarco said with a devious grin.

C knew DeMarco was up to something, he just didn't know what.

Michelle walked up to DeMarco. "Is everything good, daddy?"

"Oh yeah, he's good money. It's a small world. He said he was locked up with one of my homeboys before."

Michelle believed everything he said. DeMarco told her to take his keys and to call him when she got near his crib.

"Daddy, please don't take long."

"Gotcha, girl."

DeMarco was feeling a little nice himself. He looked to the other side of the VIP section and saw one of his ex-shorties, Tosha. He couldn't stand her anymore because she had a big mouth. He watched her from the corner of his eye and mumbled to himself, "Slick bitch," and took two more sips. Then he told Rah and Jazz he was ready to cut out.

Killer C and Cash were waiting at the front door when Jazz pulled the car up.

DeMarco came out with his two boys and jumped in the front seat. "Yo, C, make sure y'all get home in one piece."

"You know that."

"A'ight, I see y'all in the a.m."

DeMarco and his two cousins pulled off. Rah was in the backseat knocked out.

A little while later, Jazz pulled up to DeMarco's crib and saw DeMarco's chicks outside waiting for him.

"I'm saying, cuz, your chicks don't play."

"I mean, what can I say?"

Jazz took off as Michelle, Tia, and Kee-Kee followed DeMarco inside.

Michelle walked into DeMarco's bedroom, but came right back out. "So, whose hair is this? What, you have a white girl in here or something?"

DeMarco thought to himself how India got that Indian hair and some must have fallen on his bed. "Girl, don't play with me. You know what to do," he replied.

A few seconds later, all of them were naked. Kee-Kee passed DeMarco the blunt. He lit it and took a puff. Michelle sat right on his dick. She was going up and down while Tia was kissing on his neck as Kee-Kee began sucking Tia's titties.

DeMarco looked at the girls and decided to do something different. He searched inside the closet and returned with a video camera.

"What, we makin porn or somethin?" Michelle asked.

"Yes we are," he said with a grin.

He started filming them fucking each other. The tape was just for insurance in case one of them ever got out of line. They were so caught up in the moment they didn't care why he was doing it.

The next day, the whole town was talking about Skip's party. DeMarco was up early talking with Skip.

"So, DeMarco, what do you want us to do with this dude Body? We just saw him in the Pancake House."

"See what he's tryna spend and let him hustle in New River. But keep your eyes on him."

"Okay, cool. Say no more."

CHAPTER NINETEEN

After a month or so, DeMarco started thinking Body was a good dude. Body began hanging out with Skip and the crew. His cousin Black was sick when he found out Body was fucking with them.

One day Black and his crew pulled up to the park where everybody hung out on Sundays. You could tell he'd lost all of his power, because nobody moved. In the past, you would have thought it was Deebo from *Friday* coming.

"Yo, Body, what's witcha?"

"Wassup with me? What it look like? I'm getting money and shit. I don't fuck with your ass no more, family or not."

Black didn't realize that Body knew he'd stolen most of that money from those Ohio cats. "Oh, that's how you feel, cuz?"

"Listen, man, you and this rat nigga got two minutes to get outta here before I take ya head off ya shoulders."

"Yeah, whatever, Body, we supposed to be family. You be back!"

"Nah, you better hope *you* make it back. All that money you stole from me!" he yelled.

Black walked away, knowing he'd fucked up. The only real help he had wasn't fucking with him anymore.

The whole crew started going out together every week. The more money they made, the more they partied, and now Body would do anything to show DeMarco his loyalty. One night, DeMarco approached Body after the club and told him he'd give him $25,000 to hit up Black and Man-Man.

"You don't have to kill him, but I want somebody in a wheelchair."

Body couldn't wait to get the money in his hands before DeMarco even gave the lowdown. "I got this. Give me two days and it's done."

DeMarco told him he had to fly up to New York to give LaLa some more money for the condo he had just gotten for her. "So by the time I come back, I want to hear about it."

"I got you, my nigga. I won't let you down."

From that night on, Body started watching Black's every move.

On the day of Black's son's birthday party, Body and his two homeboys jumped out of the bushes dressed in black, with stocking caps over their faces. They let off about fifty shots, hitting Black and three of his crew.

Body and his boys slipped back in the woods like thieves in the night.

"Well done," Body said with a devilish smirk.

DeMarco was lying next to his daughter when LaLa handed him his beeper and phone. Both of them were going off at the same time. He looked at his phone and saw it was Michelle, so he switched it off because he didn't want LaLa to know it was a chick on the phone. When he looked at his beeper and saw *911,* he got off the bed quietly and went into the bathroom. After the third ring, Michelle picked up.

"Daddy, where are you?"

"Wassup? Talk to me."

"Daddy, do you know some niggas from Ohio shot my brother and killed his friends? The doctor said my brother won't be able to walk again and three of his homeboys are dead."

"Damn, ma, that's crazy." He sat on the phone listening to Michelle running off at the mouth about everything, but in the back of his mind he knew his mission had been accomplished. "You good?" he asked.

"Yeah, I'm good, daddy, just wanna see you."

"Okay, listen, I'm up top, but I'll be back in two days. I'll call you as soon as I wake up, okay?"

"Make sure you do."

DeMarco moved to the living room and lit up the half-blunt in the ashtray. While he thought about his next move, he said to himself, *One down and two to go.*

* * *

The next morning DeMarco, LaLa, and Nia went to meet the realtor to give him the rest of the money for the condo.

"Hi, how are you doing, Mr. and Mrs. Jones?"

"Okay," they answered.

"Mr. Jones, my name is James Watson, and like I told your wife, it will cost $250,000 for the condo. I need $25,000 for the down payment and you have to pay the first two months of the maintenance fees."

LaLa passed Mr. Watson the money. He wrote her a receipt and gave her the keys.

"Well, Mr. and Mrs. Jones, I hope you all enjoy the place. Nice doing business with you. Make sure you take care of that pretty little baby."

"Okay, thanks again, Mr. Watson."

"No problem."

LaLa was so excited. All she ever wanted DeMarco to do was get her out of those projects. DeMarco left them and went to check on his cousins Money and Lefty, to see what had been going on since he'd been gone.

He pulled up on the block and saw Money and Tonya sitting on the porch.

"Hey, Money, look at your cousin, Mr. Babymaker himself." Tonya hadn't seen DeMarco in quite some time.

"I know y'all ain't talkin, lovebirds. Money, why you sittin all quiet?"

"You play too much, DeMarco."

Money came down off the porch and he and De-Marco walked down the block.

"Yo, DeMarco, I can't lie to you. Shit has been lookin good around here lately. It's like we got all the fiends in Queens and your boys Lefty, Sholomy, and Rye got the projects doing their numbers."

"I can't even front, that's what I've been waitin to hear. Let me tell you somethin, Money, you know how I play. Ever since we was little, I play for keeps. We need all the niggas we can get over here. 'Cause when I tell you I got it, I got it! I get enough coke to supply all of Queens. Trust me. You gonna see. When I come back, just be ready."

"You leavin already? You just got here!"

"Yeah, I had to take care of some shit with LaLa, but don't worry, I'll be back real soon. Whatever y'all doin, keep on doin it and get that bread."

"I don't know what's goin on down there, but be careful, cuz."

"Come on, Money, you know how I do."

DeMarco went back to LaLa's house to spend the rest of the night with her and his daughter; he knew this would be their last night staying at the place. LaLa and De-Marco made love all night long until the sun came up. He had to leave at 6 a.m. to beat the traffic, so he got up and walked over to his daughter's crib to give her a kiss.

"Come here, girl. Trust me, I won't let you down." He hugged and kissed them both before walking out.

He got back at 3:30 in the afternoon and it was hot as

hell. DeMarco stepped into the house and put his bags down. C was the first person he called.

"Wassup, DeMarco?"

"Man, same old shit."

"Where you at? You back?"

"Yeah, I'm in the crib. I got to go to court in the mornin."

"Oh yeah, I forgot, I saw your bail bondsman joint at the gas station. She said she was tryin to holla at you, but you wasn't answerin your phone."

"C, you know how it is when I'm with LaLa, she's like Inspector Gadget."

"Word!"

"So what's goin on with you and shorty?"

"Everything good. We moved out to the country. I couldn't do that staying-behind-the-police-department shit for too long."

"I feel you. Wassup with Skip and Bizzy? Colg?"

"Everybody's good. Niggas been layin low because the boys were ridin hard ever since that shit happened to son and them."

"Okay, cool. I'ma get up wit you later, I have to call this bail bondsman chick." DeMarco hung up and called India.

"Where you been?" she asked.

"I lost my phone."

"Do you know you have court?"

"Yeah, I know."

"Well, do you know they goin to drop the charges tomorrow?"

"Who told you that?"

"Come on, boy, I know everything. I know that when you get out of court tomorrow, you better come to my office and give me some of that fine-ass dick. Just make sure you have $6,000 for court costs."

"Why you think they gonna drop the charges?"

"Well, your lawyer called me and said they know if you go to trial you could beat it. The state doesn't like to waste money. Then one of the witnesses got killed by some dudes from Ohio."

"Damn, girl, you know everything!"

"I sure do. Well, I'll see you in court."

"I'll be there, girl."

DeMarco went into his room, dropped to his knees, and thanked God for what he'd just heard.

The next morning, DeMarco met up with his lawyer, Mr. Vanzetta.

"Hey, how have you been, Mr. Jones?"

"To tell you the truth, Mr. Vanzetta, I can't complain."

"That's good to hear. So, are you ready for court?"

"Yes I am."

"Well, we should be in and out because the DA has decided to drop all charges. All you have to do is pay court costs, if you have it."

"Yeah, I got it."

"Next, the court calls Mr. DeMarco Jones. Can I have the attorney and the DA approach the bench, please?"

DeMarco was sitting there wondering what the hell

they were talking about for so long. Finally his lawyer and the DA walked back to their respective tables. The judge looked at DeMarco and said, "Mr. Jones, do you realize that you could have killed someone that night?"

"Yes sir," he replied.

"While the state has decided to drop all the charges against you, we are giving you six months to stay out of trouble." The court officer gave DeMarco a waiver to sign. "Before you leave, stop by the window and pay your court costs or an arrest warrant will be issued. Do you understand that?"

"Yes sir."

"Do you have anything else to say?"

"No, Your Honor."

"Court is dismissed."

DeMarco couldn't wait to get out of there. "Mr. Vanzetta, thank you very much."

"No problem, Mr. Jones, and thanks for paying me the fee. Your Aunt Sheena brought it to the office yesterday."

"You're welcome."

DeMarco headed over to India's office to let her know that they had in fact dismissed his case.

"Hey, little boy!"

"Little boy? Shit, you wasn't sayin that last time you was at my house."

India closed the blinds to the office and pulled her pants down.

"Damn, India, why can't you wait till you come out to my house later?"

"I don't know what it is, but every time I see you I want to take you apart; so come on, give me some."

"Whatever!"

"I know you're gonna hurry up before my man comes back."

She bent over and DeMarco started rubbing the tip of his dick on the edge of her pussy, trying to get it nice and wet. Then he slid it right in. Pump after pump, DeMarco quickly had India moaning and screaming at the top of her lungs.

"This is how you like it?"

"Yeah, don't stop! Pull my hair!"

DeMarco grabbed her hair while hitting her big ass. When India came all over him, he was sweating like he'd been sitting inside of a sauna.

"So call me later, if you don't mind."

"A'ight," he said before fixing his clothes and leaving.

DeMarco headed straight to his cousin's house. As he pulled up to the house he saw Colg and Gee outside smoking a blunt.

"Let me find out I'm just in time," he said through the window.

"Yes you are, my nigga."

"Yo, what it is, my nigga? I told you to put your feet up, Gee."

"Well, I gotta make a move back down Miami way."

"Yeah, but I left you ten."

"When I come back we gon' really split it up."

DeMarco's expression turned serious. "How long will it be for some of that?"

"A couple of days," Gee responded.

"Okay, no problem."

When Gee drove off, Colg looked at DeMarco like he was a genius, then they moved inside the crib.

"Listen, man, like I told you before, Gee fucks with you and we the only niggas he trusts down here."

DeMarco took Colg's truck and went to stash the work, but this time in town. His first stop was the mall.

"Oh shit, wassup, DeMarco?"

"What's good, Body?"

"I can't complain."

DeMarco hadn't seen Body since he put that work in for him. Body was now one of DeMarco's top shooters.

"Body, what you doin in here?"

"I told you, my little joint work in here. She work at Victoria's Secret."

"Oh yeah, you did say that."

"I know Killer C and Skip told you I've been doin my numbers."

"Come on, Body, you know I like that. You turned out to be a good dude."

"I told you that night at the club that I'm a real nigga. I'm not with that pussy shit Black was on."

"Yeah, I see that. Good lookin on that thing too."

"Anytime. All you gotta do is line 'em up and I'll shoot 'em down."

DeMarco reached inside his pocket and passed Body $5,000. "Keep our BI. Plus, I'll have somethin else for you real soon."

"DeMarco, you don't have to worry about me. I'm the real deal, hit me up whenever."

DeMarco walked to the other side of the mall and found Kee-Kee standing in front of the pet store.

"What you doin, girl?"

"I was just lookin in the window tryna decide if I should buy me this pretty-ass dog or not."

"Which dog?"

"This little Yorkie."

"What do they want for it?"

"The man said he would give it to me for $1,500."

"Here, go get it," he said, pullin out $2,000.

"No, DeMarco! You really gonna get it for me?" she asked in shock.

"The money's right here."

DeMarco waited outside and she came out ten minutes later with the dog, happy as hell.

"Thanks, daddy!"

"You already know. I'm sayin, do you wanna make some real money?"

"Daddy, you know I'm down for anythin."

"Okay, cool, that nigga Body is down by Foot Locker. Go over there and get his number. Act like you gonna give him some pussy."

"DeMarco, you know that nigga is crazy!"

"Not like me."

"Okay, I'll do it."

"Meet me at my crib later and make sure you come by yourself."

"Okay."

Later that night Kee-Kee did as told and came to his crib. DeMarco had always wanted to fuck Kee-Kee's little brown-skinned ass by himself anyway. They smoked and fucked all over his house. He must have bust three or four nuts that night. After they finished, he put her up on the plan. Her eyes got bigger and bigger because all she saw were dollar signs.

"Kee-Kee, you better not say anything to Michelle either."

She let him know that she really didn't like that bitch anyway because she slept with her baby pops. The more she talked, the more he saw her true colors starting to come out.

"Well, you can stay here tonight if you want to." DeMarco knew he had to keep her close for his plan to work.

"Daddy, I want you to do somethin to me that I ain't never done before. I want you to fuck me in my ass."

"In your ass? Girl, my dick can't fit in there."

"Yes it can, I bought something especially for that. It's Astroglide. Come on, daddy, let's try it."

DeMarco squirted the stuff on his dick and some in Kee-Kee's ass. After a few attempts, his dick went right in.

"Damn, girl, that shit really work."

Kee-Kee didn't say a word. All she could do was concentrate and back that ass up on him. She was cumming and licking her nipples at the same time.

"Do you like that, daddy?"

DeMarco couldn't believe what she was doing. She was feeling on her pussy while his dick stayed in her ass.

They both fell asleep on the couch, exhausted.

DeMarco woke up and noticed his cousin Colg had called him a few times.

"Yo, Colg, what's good?"

"I called you a few times."

"Man, I was asleep. I had a rough night."

"Your boy Gee is back. He said he'll be around like 8:00."

"Okay, cool."

After ending the call, DeMarco went to see his man Killer C.

"Yo, C, come outside."

"Okay, I'll be right there."

Five minutes later, C jumped in the car. "What's good, DeMarco?"

"I have somethin I need you to do for me later, so make sure you around, and bring Body wit you. Matter of fact, I'll go get him myself."

"Okay, he's at shorty from the mall's crib."

"She lives in that pink and green house, right?"

"Yeah, that's the one."

Moments later, DeMarco called his cousin Colg to take care of his business with Gee, although he didn't know it would be the last time. "Colg, I'm on my way to-bring you the money for Gee because I'm about to leave town."

Less than twenty minutes later, DeMarco pulled up to his cousin's house with the money. He gave Colg the duffel bag and said, "Yo, it's all there, take your cut, make sure Gee gets the rest and lay low for a few days." He gave him a hug and headed straight to his spot. He got to his stash house, loaded his trunk and backseat with work, cash, and the other things he needed. Once the car was loaded, he drove to I-95, praying he didn't get stopped on his way back to New York.

Kee-Kee called Body and he picked up on the first ring.

"Wassup, baby?" Kee-Kee said.

"Ain't shit. I'm about to go up to VA for a couple days. You wanna come wit me, girl?"

"Yeah, I'll go, just give me an hour and I'll meet you."

CHAPTER TWENTY

Killer C was waiting on his porch. DeMarco had given them the rundown and told C when to make his next move. Body was on the way to come pick Kee-Kee up.

"What's takin you so long to come outta the house?" Body asked her over the phone when he arrived.

"I have to get some clothes," she said.

"Girl, you don't need clothes. You with Big Body the Don!"

Kee-Kee and Body drove for about two hours before Body pulled into a gas station. He hadn't noticed Killer C following him. When he pulled back into the traffic, he felt a bump.

"I know this nigga didn't hit my car?" he said.

Body got out of the car and walked over to the vehicle behind him. He knocked on the window and Killer C rolled it down, letting off one shot. He hit Body in the forehead and drove off. Kee-Kee jumped into the driver's seat and followed Killer C back onto the highway. They drove to the next town over and parked the car. Kee-Kee went to the trunk of Body's car and pulled out the big bag. Killer C poured gas all over the car and set fire to it.

About eleven hours later, Killer C and Kee-Kee pulled up to the block in Queens where DeMarco was parked on the opposite side of the street, waiting. DeMarco opened the trunk of his car and C couldn't believe his eyes. There were thirty bricks and so much cash it would take all day to count.

"I can't lie, DeMarco, you are the best that ever did it!"

"Tell Kee-Kee to come here."

She was still a little shaken up from what had happened.

"Kee-Kee, you good?" DeMarco asked.

She was just stuck in a daze, holding the big black bag in her hand.

"Kee-Kee, you can have whatever is in that bag."

She didn't know what was in it, so she quickly unzipped it. When she saw all of that cash inside, she was so happy—all she ever wanted to do was have enough cash to take care of her son. "Thank you, daddy." Tears of joy rolled down her cheeks.

DeMarco still had a lot of money in the streets of North Carolina and he told Killer C that whatever was down there, he could have.

"Good lookin! But what are you sayin?"

"What I'm sayin is, I'm done with that place."

C and Kee-Kee got back in the car to head back south to North Carolina.

"I love you, daddy," Kee-Kee said, putting her seat belt on.

From that day on, DeMarco never went back down there again. As he drove off, he yelled out to them, "You ain't see me!"

This was DeMarco's first day back in the Big Apple. LaLa didn't know he was there yet; he wanted to surprise her. LaLa and her mother were moving the last bit of her stuff into the new condo. When she opened the door, she felt like things had been moved around. She walked into the back room and pushed the door open slowly to find DeMarco lying on the bed, out like a light. His bags were spread out everywhere.

"Baby, wake up. Why didn't you call me and tell me you were back?"

DeMarco looked like he'd just had a serious dream. "Oh shit, girl, you scared me."

"Like I said, why didn't you call me?"

DeMarco told her to sit down beside him.

"Well, I'm waiting."

"Girl, I was tired. I had a long night and I been up for like two days."

"What's all this stuff and all these garbage bags?"

"Check it out yourself."

She began opening up bag after bag and couldn't believe how much cash and coke he had. Thinking to herself, *This crazy nigga must have robbed a bank or somethin.*

"Well, LaLa, I'm back. I kept thinkin about what you were sayin when I was up here last time. So I decided to leave that South shit behind. I love you and my daughter to death."

"Where did you get all of this coke from?"

"Man, stop askin all of these questions. Just know that we good."

"Let me get outta here before my mother comes in. And I hope you ain't leaving all of this stuff in here?"

"Nah, I'm about to go find a storage unit."

Finally, DeMarco felt at home. He took the batteries out of his cell phone and broke his beeper in half then fell back asleep.

The next morning DeMarco went to pick up Money. He would know exactly where to find a storage unit.

DeMarco stayed in the car while Money went inside to handle everything.

"Yo, DeMarco, pull over to the third storage on the left."

"Money, come here and check this out."

Money opened the bags as though he'd just seen a dead body. "Oh shit, DeMarco, we on!"

"I told you, nigga, I got enough coke to cover all of Queens."

"Yo, DeMarco, I'm gonna keep it tall wit you, I thought you was talkin just to be talkin."

"Come on, Money, don't even try to play me like that."

Money couldn't wait to hit the streets and get this money. He had so many customers, but never had the weight they all needed. "Man, DeMarco, we gon' make a killin off all this shit."

DeMarco knew that it was a whole different ball game the way niggas played in New York. "Money, I need to go buy a hooptie from somewhere. Plus, I wanna go check my man that make the fake licenses."

"What kind are you trying to buy?"

"One that cost about $4,000."

"I hear that. What about your other cars?"

"We'll bring them out when needed. We gotta get out here in these streets and see who is who."

See, you had some heavy hitters from Queens, like Big Dog and a crew called Prime Team, and DeMarco and Money were still the new niggas. DeMarco didn't wanna make any mistakes at all.

Money pulled into the used-car lot and as soon as they walked inside, DeMarco's eyes were on the oldest car in the spot, an all-black Ford Taurus with tints.

"How much you want for that Taurus?"

"I'll give it to you for $3,800."

DeMarco was a businessman. "I'll give you $3,500 right now and if you have something else like this I might be able to give you $7,000."

"Give me a second." The guy walked inside and came back fast, throwing DeMarco the keys to the Taurus. "What do you think about a gray Chevy?"

DeMarco nodded.

"Can you give me a few minutes to clean them out?"

"Nah, you don't have to do that," DeMarco said. "We'll take 'em just the way they are. We'll take one now and come back later for the other one."

DeMarco had a guy who used to put the stash boxes in his Uncle Bruh's cars. So he went straight to the shop, dropped the Taurus off, then headed back and got the Chevy.

"Yo, DeMarco, I haven't seen you in years. You a big man now."

DeMarco hadn't seen Dave since he used to hustle for his uncle. "Word."

"What can I help you with?"

"You know what I need and I also want some plates and insurance."

"DeMarco, give me three days and I'll have you on the road."

"Sounds cool to me."

DeMarco gave him $6,000 and got back into the car with Money. Money was sitting there remembering how DeMarco had run away from the Tryon Residential Center not that long ago, and had started working for his mother and his Aunt V. *Look how fast this nigga blew up!*

Money and DeMarco were running around making their rounds.

"Before we do anything else, we gotta go check my nigga Chief."

Chief was in the bar doing what he liked to do: popping bottles and talking shit.

"Ayo, Chief, what's good, stranger?"

"Damn, little nigga, look at that, you forgot about a nigga."

"Never that, I just had to take care of a few things, but now I'm back up here for good."

"Shit, I told niggas you was one of the smart ones. I'm sayin, DeMarco, talk about it."

DeMarco started putting Chief onto what he was trying to do, but not letting him know how many bricks he actually had.

"DeMarco, you know you my little homey. However the ball bounce, that's good. I got a lot of blocks for you."

"Chief, on some real shit, let's do it."

Chief popped a bottle of Moët and poured DeMarco a glass. "A toast to gettin more money."

Chief and DeMarco put their glasses to the sky and said, "More money!" at the same time.

When they got back to the block at 5, Lefty and his niggas were out there.

"Oh, that's how you doin it now? DeMarco, you back and don't holla at your boy?"

"Lefty, you know I don't kiss and tell. I'm here, ain't I?" he replied.

"DeMarco, these are my homeys, real niggas."

"Wassup?"

"Ain't shit, DeMarco. We heard a lot about you from your cousin."

"I mean, ain't nothin to it but to do it. Lefty, come back at like 11:30 and we can do what it do."

DeMarco went upstairs to check on his aunts Momma Paula and Aunt V.

"Hey, boy, how you been doing?"

"I been fine."

"So what brings you back up here?"

"I had to come back, LaLa was having a fit. Saying stuff like I haven't been spending time with my daughter."

"Well, you brought her into the world, so you have to be a father."

"Look who the wind blew in," Aunt V. said.

It was Steph. "Come and give me a hug, boy, you know I'm mad at you!"

"Why, man?"

"You just left me up here for dead."

"Hell no I didn't! I had to bust some moves, you know it ain't even like that."

After they set up shop and time went on, DeMarco started having niggas from all over Queens checking him. From Merrick, Baisley, 40 projects, and even niggas from LeFrak. Shit started getting bigger than he'd ever imagined. Some of his blocks were doing $30,000 a day off straight bagged-up work; everybody was trying to get down with his team. He wouldn't let anybody in if they didn't start day one with him. Period. Niggas couldn't understand how he and his crew never ran out of work—even some of his crew wondered, but they never asked questions. The only one who knew was Money, and he would never break the code of silence to anyone.

CHAPTER TWENTY-ONE

It was the night of Chief's birthday party. DeMarco and all his crew met up and headed to JB's spot. Shit was wall to wall; every chick you could name was out. DeMarco and his homeboys were at the bar doing what they did best, when some shorty walked to the opposite side and just stared at DeMarco, trying to get his attention.

"Bartender, can you please give that guy with the NY Mets hat my number and whatever he's drinkin?"

The bartender walked up to DeMarco and did what she had asked. DeMarco thought to himself, *Not again.* She did look really familiar, but he couldn't remember how he knew her.

"Bartender, I'll tell you what, you keep the drink and I'll keep the number," DeMarco said.

"No problem."

She sat in the same spot and watched DeMarco all night long. DeMarco had to ask his homeboy, JB where she was from. JB let him know that Tammy was from Baisley and she hung out with LaLa. Then, DeMarco remembered one time he had a girl in his crib and somebody told LaLa—it was shorty who had gone with LaLa to jump the girl.

DeMarco was sitting there puzzled, wondering why she would give him her number. It didn't take a rocket scientist to figure it out, but he still wasn't taking any chances just in case LaLa had put her up to it.

After the party was over, he went home to find LaLa and the baby asleep on the couch. DeMarco grabbed his daughter and LaLa followed them to the bedroom. He still had the number in his pocket. He quietly took it out and slid it in the bottom of the sole of his Air Max 95.

In the morning LaLa wanted to go to the mall to get the baby's ears pierced. Ironically, they ran into Tammy.

"Hey, wassup, girl?" she greeted LaLa.

"Nothing, just came to get Boops's ears pierced. What you up to?"

"Oh, she looks just like her dad," she said, staring at DeMarco, licking her lips with a fuck-me face.

He just stood there like he didn't see her.

"Well, do you need a ride, girl? Because we about to leave anyway," said LaLa.

They all got in the car and headed toward Baisley. DeMarco kept glancing at Tammy through the rearview mirror. When they arrived at her crib, she got out of the car and kissed LaLa and the baby.

"Thanks again, and call me later, girl."

She dropped her house keys and bent down to pick them up, pointing her ass at DeMarco. Smiling at him and licking her lips as she walked into the building. De-Marco drove off, shaking his head.

Next, he wanted to check on his cousin Lefty and LaLa's mother wanted to see the baby.

"Okay, LaLa, go see your moms and I'm gonna run over to Lefty's house real quick."

"You better not be tryna holla at those chicks over there either."

"A'ight, bye."

DeMarco headed to his cousin's house and knocked on the door. After a few more knocks, Lefty finally opened up.

"Damn, Left, I was bangin for a minute."

"My fault, cuz, I was bumpin that new Biggie, *Life After Death*. That song he got with Too $hort is my type of shit." Lefty had the whole kitchen table full of black-top capsules.

"Yo, that whole idea about 'buy one and get one free' got niggas sick!"

"I told you, nigga! I knew what I was doin."

"My nigga Sholomy said he got a spot on Sutphin that he could lock down."

"I mean, do what you do 'cause I don't knock a nigga hustle."

"Word. A'ight, bet."

"I'm sayin, wassup with that chick Tammy?"

"Oh, shorty, good money, I always wanted that. She

messes with some dude across the street. Why you asked about her?"

"Because anytime I see her, she's on me. I was just with LaLa on the Ave and we dropped her off, and before that at JB's spot, she gave me her number."

"Give me her number and I'll get her over here for you right now."

Lefty immediately called her.

"Hello, who dis?"

"It's me, Lefty."

"How you get my number? And my homegirl said she not messin with you no more 'cause you fucked her sista."

"Man, I don't know what you're talkin about. Anyway, come to my house real quick. Somebody I want you to see is here."

"Who? Boy, stop playin."

"Just come here real quick."

"Okay, give me five minutes," she said, and ended the call.

"She's on the way over here now."

"Put some of that shit up," DeMarco said.

"We good. She knows what time it is."

"Lefty, you crazy."

They smoked a blunt while they waited for Tammy to arrive.

Knock knock.

"That must be shorty at the door."

Lefty let her in. When she walked into the kitchen, she couldn't believe it was DeMarco sitting in the chair.

"Wassup, shorty? Small world, huh?"

"Lefty, why you set me up?"

"Set you up? You just hit the Lotto."

"Lotto? So where my money at?"

DeMarco grabbed her hand and led her into the living room.

"So I'm sayin, don't you think you playin it a little too close?"

DeMarco didn't know how much she knew about him—LaLa used to run her mouth with her every time he went out of town. But one thing you didn't do was tell another chick about your nigga; especially if he was getting money.

"I'm not sayin that I'm not, but I liked you from the first day I laid eyes on you," Tammy told him.

"I'm saying I have to pick LaLa up from her mom's crib, but we can get up tonight. Word is you have a boyfriend."

"If that's what you call it, we gonna see about that tonight. Just call me."

The way she said that, he knew it was going down. She got up and kissed him on his cheek and walked out.

"Oh shit, LaLa's calling me."

"I'm ready to go home, DeMarco, it's getting late," LaLa said on the other end of the line.

"Make your way downstairs, I'm on my way." He hung up. "I'm out Lefty, but good lookin on that one."

"Come on, that's light, LaLa!" DeMarco yelled while she

struggled to put the baby seat in the back. All DeMarco could think about was Tammy.

"I hope you staying in tonight, babes."

"Yeah, I am," he lied.

As soon as they got to the house, DeMarco told LaLa to put the baby in the crib and to come sit on the couch with him to watch *Juice*. He knew he had to come up with a good excuse to get away for a couple hours. He started kissing on LaLa's neck, and before you know it, that was all she wrote. They were all over each other.

"Damn, boy, slow down, you tryna kill my shit."

DeMarco kept pounding that donkey out till they both fell asleep. He woke up at 10 and saw that Lefty had called him five times.

"Yo, Left, what's good."

"Where you at? Shorty was lookin for you like crazy. You definitely have a chance to hit that tonight."

"I'm on my way."

DeMarco went in the living room and told LaLa some bullshit about Lefty getting arrested, and she went for it. He grabbed his nine and headed straight to the projects to pick Tammy up. As he exited the Van Wyck, he called her but she didn't answer, but then she called right back.

"Hey, Mr. Let Me Down."

"Nah, never that. I'm comin down Linden now."

"Okay, cool, pick me up in the back of my building because it's a lot of people standin in the front."

"Got you."

As DeMarco approached the light on Guy R. Brewer,

he saw what Tammy was talking about. It looked like the whole pj's were outside. He drove past and around to the back of the building where he found her waiting. She hopped in and off they went.

"Wassup, girl?"

"Nothin. Damn, boy, what's that in your hand?"

DeMarco had on his black gloves and was holding a big nine.

"Let me see that."

"Girl, get outta here. What you gonna do with it?"

"I love guns," she said. "I wanna shoot that one day."

"Let me worry about all that; you too pretty to play wit guns."

He jumped on the highway and drove out to City Island. He threw in his Tupac *All Eyez On Me* CD and played track five. He peeked over at her and noticed how she was into the song, saying to himself, *This is my kind of chick*. They stopped at Sammy's to eat and when they got back into the car, DeMarco lit the blunt he was carrying behind his ear. He passed it to her, putting his hand on her leg while he was still driving, rubbing up and down, getting closer to her pussy. He glanced over and noticed that she didn't have any panties on and his dick got hard as a brick.

"Shorty, let me find out why you don't have no panties on."

"Boy, it's too hot for that."

"So what do you wanna do?"

"I'm wit whatever," she answered.

"So let's go somewhere to chill."

He drove to his favorite motel, the Kew Motor Inn.

As soon as they got into their room, no questions asked, Tammy jumped in the shower and he came in right behind her. Tammy had a fat ass and some nice titties with her soft caramel skin. DeMarco started kissing on her neck and rubbing on her completely shaven pussy as she was massaging his dick. He moved even closer to her and slid his dick in from behind. Her pussy was feeling so good. Without drying, they went straight to the bed, leaving all the lights on.

"Damn, boy, you are everything."

For some odd reason he felt close to her, more so than any other chick besides his baby LaLa. It was like love at first sight in every sense of the word.

Once morning came, DeMarco dropped Tammy off, handed her a $1,000, and told her to buy herself something nice. She gave him a kiss and was about to step out when she said, "You better not had got me pregnant."

"Nah, I pulled out," he quickly replied.

She knew he was lying like a motherfucker. "A'ight, call me later," she said.

"A'ight."

As soon as DeMarco started his car, he saw his cousin Money drive by. Money stopped at the light, so DeMarco pulled up next to him and rolled his window down.

"Yo, Money, where you goin?"

"Nigga, you better blow your horn or somethin. I was about to light your shit up—and you better start answerin your phone," Money said.

"I was busy last night. Wassup, though?"

"Follow me to the block. Somethin just happened."

They both jumped out of their cars as soon as they arrived.

"Yo, DeMarco, some niggas came through here lookin for you, talkin about you better shut your block down."

"So where are these supposed-to-be gangstas at?"

"They old heads from across town."

"Money, I'm gonna keep it straight up wit you: a nigga is the last thing I'm worried about. You know what block they from?"

"Hell yeah! I'm already on top of that."

"My thing is, how you gonna come to a nigga hood lookin for a nigga, but you got a hundred niggas on the block outside hustlin. Come on, Money, let's ride through there."

"Yo, park your car down the street and leave it runnin. We gon' walk down there." Money opened his stash box and pulled out his Glock 19.

"Yo, Money, I don't give a fuck who out there. We hittin everythin movin."

"I'm sayin, it's broad daylight."

"So what? That makes it even better."

When they hit the corner, DeMarco and Money started letting it go like it was the Fourth of July. Niggas and bitches were running everywhere. One dude tried to make it to the garbage can where he probably had his heat. DeMarco ran his ass down.

POW! POW! POW!

"Come look for that!"

"Yo, DeMarco, let's get outta here before somebody calls the boys."

DeMarco wasn't trying to hear that. He walked in the door of the house Money identified for him and shot some old man and his bitch, then walked right out like nothing happened. He hopped back into the car with Money, hitting the corner doing almost one hundred miles an hour.

"Money, slow this shit down! We good; the hard part is over. Now let them come look for us."

Chief got a whiff of what was going down and came to DeMarco's block mad as fuck because DeMarco hadn't told him.

"Yo, my lil' nigga, why didn't you put me on? I would have sent my niggas through there. Not saying you couldn't handle it, but I always told you there's a way of doin shit."

"I feel what you sayin, but those niggas don't know who they fuckin wit. This won't be the first or the last nigga I put a hole in."

That evening, one of DeMarco's workers got shot going to the store. He ran back to the block like he was on a track team.

"Yo, DeMarco, some nigga in a black Pathfinder shot me in the leg!"

"Which leg?"

"My right leg, can't you see?"

DeMarco pulled out his gun and shot him in the other leg.

"Now take stupid to the hospital."

Money and Chief didn't realize DeMarco was on a whole other level; he had plenty of money, so that made him even more dangerous.

For the next few days, DeMarco was all over the streets doing his homework, trying to find out anything he could about the old niggas that came to his block. One night he and Tammy were leaving Lefty's house when she got the word that the baby mother of one of the old dudes was in the salon on the boulevard getting her hair done.

It was a hot summer night and there were people everywhere. DeMarco parked his car by the side of the salon and grabbed his nine out of his stash box.

"Hold on, DeMarco, let me do it."

"Girl, chill out."

"No, I'm serious, they would never suspect a girl walkin up in there."

DeMarco and Tammy were hanging out hard, so he knew she was serious.

"Okay, cool. Listen, when you go in there, walk right up on her and give her ass the business. You gotta make sure you don't give anyone else eye contact—"

Tammy jumped out of the car before he could finish talking. DeMarco thought to himself, *This bitch is crazy*. Tammy was definitely his kind of chick.

She walked right up to the girl, who was sitting in the second chair and let off five shots like she was a professional. Tammy hit her in the chest, neck, and head. Everybody dropped to the floor and stayed there. For good measure, before leaving, she fired one more shot into the ceiling and walked out.

"Come on baby, we out. Let them talk about it."

"So what happened?"

"It happened. That's what happened," Tammy said, lighting up a blunt she had rolled on the way down there. DeMarco knew from that night on that she was Bonnie and he was Clyde.

After they pulled away, Tammy looked over to him and said, "And by the way, I'm four months pregnant."

DeMarco couldn't believe what he'd just heard, but in his heart, he loved Tammy and he told her so. She definitely had to keep their baby.

"Listen, we gonna take a trip to the Poconos for a few days and let the smoke clear."

"Okay, baby daddy, whatever you wanna do," she agreed.

Late that night, they took the trip and got there about 6 in the morning. Both of them so exhausted, they lay across the bed and went to sleep with their clothes on.

DeMarco woke up after a long sleep and saw Tammy sitting in a chair smoking a blunt like nothing ever happened.

"Wassup, girl? You up early."

"Clyde, what you talking about *early?* Do you know it's 3 in the afternoon?"

DeMarco sat on the couch next to her and laid on

her lap smoking a blunt. He looked up at her, thinkin about his next move.

"Come on, boy, pass me the blunt . . . The blunt!"

"Ain't you pregnant?" He wasn't letting his child come into this world unhealthy.

CHAPTER TWENTY-TWO

Chief called a meeting at their usual spot. The whole team pulled up one by one. He wanted to put everything in proper perspective.

"DeMarco, check this out, my nigga. You are gettin too much money to be out here chasin ghosts. You let niggas chase *you* and that's the bottom line. Word is, niggas don't even know who slumped shorty, so in other words that's a free one."

Chief was the nigga who knew everythin and had all the bosses scared of him.

"And for the rest of you niggas, if crack is sold on any other block or crack spot, we want in on it. When it comes to beef shit, let me handle that."

One night, DeMarco and his crew were in the gambling spot. DeMarco must've won about $30,000. Lefty walked in while he was talking shit about a bet. DeMarco had kind of fallen back from Lefty because he started putting shit in the game by selling his own work. Since he didn't fuck with Lefty like that anymore, he left the spot to hit the gun stash.

He jumped into his drop-top BMW, with his top shooter Murder, heading to the projects where Lefty kept the guns. The two of them went inside the apartment and took all the guns stashed there, but they noticed that the .44 Bulldog was gone.

"Yo, I bet my life that he had that .44 on him. That's why he was acting cocky like that."

"You right, DeMarco, I think he mad because you ain't fuckin with him no more."

As they were walking out of the building, they noticed Lefty and some Spanish chick pulling up. When Lefty got out of the car, Murder pulled out his .357 long.

"Nah, Murder, I got this." DeMarco walked up to Lefty. "I'm sayin."

"You sayin what, nigga? You ready to die?" Lefty reached for the .44 at his waist, but before he could get it out, DeMarco shot him in the leg, just to teach him a lesson of why not to fuck with the boss.

Over the next couple of months, DeMarco started fucking with Lefty's homeboys Sholomy and Rye. Car after car, chain after chain, you name it, them boys had it. Pretty soon the niggas in the projects started getting jealous of DeMarco and his crew. For one, he wasn't from over there and the niggas they grew up with were fucking with him. To top it off, he had babies by two of the baddest chicks from over there. He was the go-to man.

One night while DeMarco was over there parked in his truck, he peeped two niggas with black Champion hoodies standing in front of the building looking suspicious. He cocked his nines and put one in each pocket.

One of the guys said, "I see you, outlaw."

DeMarco looked at both of them and smiled while shooting them in their stomachs, then he took their guns. He went into the building and walked upstairs to link with his man Capone. They were somewhat the same: both of them were wild and had baby mothers from Baisley, but didn't live there. The two together were nothing to play with. He also had a Spanish homeboy from over there named Nut that was like O-Dog from *Menace II Society*.

One early morning, about a week later, DeMarco woke up and thought he thought he was dreaming. He put a pillow over his head and thought to himself, *Let me try this again*. When he removed the pillow, he discovered he wasn't dreaming. He couldn't believe his eyes—his son and daughter were laying there with him. He jumped out of bed, picked them both up, and walked into the living room. There he saw LaLa, Tammy, and K sitting at the table sipping on some E&J Cask & Cream.

"Yo, what the hell is going on?"

"Shit, what you thought? I wasn't gonna find out?" LaLa said with a big smile on her face.

DeMarco was stuck; he had to sit before he fell down with the kids in his arms. He had a lot of chicks, but he never imagined anything like this before. He sat there for a minute; it felt like when the judge had sentenced him to eighteen months in Tryon.

"Well, you gonna say anythin?" LaLa asked. When he didn't respond, she continued: "Since the cat got your tongue, I been heard that you got my best friend pregnant; you know the streets talk. When I called her, she kept it real with me. Not saying it didn't hurt, but I love her so much, I want the same thing for her that I want for myself. At the end of the day, I'm a real bitch and real bitches do real things!"

Tammy sat there quietly because she knew she'd been dead wrong to get pregnant by her best friend's man. For a minute, DeMarco didn't say anything either because he knew he was dead wrong too. He just sat there looking at them. Then, he said, "I'll be right back, I gotta run to the car real quick."

As soon as he got to the car, he pulled out the blunt that he stashed behind the glove box. He sat there thinking about how he was the don of all dons. But he snapped back into reality when he realized that he was now responsible for two lives. When he went back inside, they were laughing like nothing ever happened.

"Okay, everybody into the living room," DeMarco ordered. "You too K, you probably ran your mouth too."

K was always around Tammy and she was the type of chick who believed in God and felt like the truth would always set you free. Not saying she didn't do her dirt, but that's how she was.

"Check this out, since everything is out in the open,

I'm just gonna let y'all know that I love y'all both to death. I'm gonna take care of my kids and buy both of y'all a crib and a whip in two weeks."

Tammy and LaLa just looked at each other and smiled.

DeMarco had been laying low for a minute since he shot his cousin and what happened in the salon. One day, he decided to finally go to the hood and check on his other cousin Money. He pulled up on the block and saw Money sitting on the porch with like ten niggas.

Money heard loud music and knew it had to be De-Marco, because he was the only nigga in the hood with a system like that. You could hear it from blocks away.

DeMarco rolled his window down. "Yo, Money, wassup?"

"Shit, you tell me, where you been at, son?"

"A nigga had to take a break," DeMarco said.

Tonya was sitting on the porch with an ice grill like she wanted to kill DeMarco with her bare hands. They jumped into Money's car and headed to the projects.

"Yo, DeMarco, there go your man Rye right there hollering at that chick."

"Pull over," DeMarco said.

As soon as they stepped out, all eyes were on them. DeMarco and Money were strapped up, so they didn't give a fuck.

"Damn, DeMarco, where you been at? You pulled a Makaveli on us," Rye said, surprised.

"Come on, let's go upstairs."

Shortly after, DeMarco followed Money and Rye to one of Sholomy's chick's cribs.

"Yo, what the fuck is that?" he asked.

"Oh, that's Kong, my pitbull."

"I'm saying, what's good over here?"

"Same ol' shit, you know we always gonna get that cash."

"Yo, show DeMarco how we play."

"Excuse me, y'all gotta get up for a sec."

Rye pulled out close to $60,000 from under a cushion.

"Okay, I see it's like that. I'm sayin, how many niggas y'all got workin for y'all?"

"Not too many."

"Word? And y'all still gettin it like that?"

"If you want to come over here with us, it's up to you, DeMarco. The ball is in your court."

DeMarco knew that Money had Merrick on lock and didn't want to step on his toes; he just felt that there were too many workers selling two-for-five's and he didn't really press it because they were all from over there.

"How much do they pay their workers?"

"I think thirty off a hundred."

"That's it? Cool, we just gonna put ours in fifty-fifty and we gonna give them fifty off a hundred. That's how we gonna kill the game and sell weight only to those we fuck with."

"So as of now, I need y'all to come with me outside and show me who is who."

Within two weeks, they had the projects on lock too. All

the young niggas were fucking with DeMarco and his team. Dice games, chuck-a-luck parties, fucking all types of bitches, and shoot-outs, you name it; shit was feeling like Queens again!

DeMarco had chicks all over the projects and even had bitches from 40 coming to Baisley—and 40 and Baisley projects hated each other. DeMarco had keys to all of the chicks' apartments like he was the rent office.

DeMarco was driving down the block when he saw Sha Dilly, a dude he knew. He stopped and rolled down his window. "Yo, wassup, shorty?"

"Ain't shit, just came from a dice game across the street."

DeMarco had a weakness for rolling dice because he hardly ever lost. He had one of the best arms in Queens. "It's money in the bank?"

"Hell yeah!"

"Hold on, let me park."

"Yo, DeMarco, if you got somethin on you, keep it in the car because the boys been riding hard," Sha Dilly warned.

"Good lookin." DeMarco put both of his nines under the seat and closed his door.

As they crossed the street, DeMarco heard the door close in back of the building. Being that it was dark out, he couldn't see well. As his eyes adjusted, he saw a nigga in a black mask with a shotgun in his hand. What saved DeMarco's life was that he had the heart of a lion. He threw shorty on the ground and kept walking toward

him. "I'm sayin, if you gonna bust that shit, bust it."
He just kept both of his hands in his pockets, repeating,
"Bust that shit, bust it." He heard a voice coming from
under the mask say, "Yo, this nigga crazy!" He automati-
cally picked up on it and thought, *Oh, this nigga.*

The dude finally let off two shots and ran.

DeMarco checked his body to make sure he wasn't
hit. He flew to his car and grabbed his two nines with
the extended clips. No questions asked, he walked back
across the street, straight to the dice game.

"All you muthafuckers, get on the ground!"

DeMarco took his black skully off, then ordered the
others to take off *everything* and fill it up with their shit.
Niggas were scared to death. One even tried to run. De-
Marco shot at him and the guy immediately stopped in
his tracks.

The next day, that shit was the talk of the projects. De-
Marco reasoned that since everyone would think he was
going to lay low, it would be the perfect time for him and
his crew to be outside early in the morning to catch anybody else trying to sell product.

A chick from across the street walked past DeMarco
and his crew.

"Come here, shorty, take this $200 and let me walk
wit you."

Shorty didn't know what was going on, but she
wasn't about to turn down the cash. DeMarco noticed a
few niggas standing in the doorway of the building. He
pulled his shit out and let off fifteen shots at them.

"Pussy asses, don't run now!" DeMarco said under his breath.

Shorty was scared senseless even as her pussy got wet—she couldn't believe how calm and smooth he'd done that.

DeMarco ran with both of his guns, showing them he meant business. He told his crew to meet him in the park.

"This is how we gonna do this since these niggas want to play with the kid. We gonna do twenty-four-hour shifts and whoever we catch out here hustlin, we straight up takin they shit. I'm gonna bring some of my niggas from Merrick over here to hold y'all down."

DeMarco, Murder, and Capone had all the bitches on their dicks. They would go from apartment to apartment fucking those chicks. DeMarco even got caught in a staircase getting head from his man C-Black's mom. Shit was off the hook. Niggas used to come back and tell his crew all types of shit, sell them guns, and do packs for them. What made DeMarco that nigga to them was that he took care of his whole team. They all had cars, motorcycles, big jewels, and a lot of money, which brought the shorties. This made niggas talk shit, but they were scared to death of DeMarco and his crew.

They had niggas so scared, they started calling the police on them. DeMarco was the type to be out there for two to three months and then suddenly disappear. He got the word that little niggas were talking saying that LaLa's and Tammy's babies' father was robbing and shooting mad niggas.

DeMarco, Murder, and Capone were on their way down the hill when the cops pulled up on them in a blue van. One officer looked over to DeMarco and commanded them to stop.

"Where are you going? Show me your IDs and please step out of the vehicle."

DeMarco got out and went into his pocket like he was going for his ID, then took off running. One cop went after him and the other pulled his gun on Murder and Capone.

DeMarco knew Baisley projects like the back of his hand. As he entered building four, he slammed and locked the door. He hurried to his man Nut's house to stash his guns and laid low until the police left from in front of the building.

The cops were so mad that DeMarco got away that they beat the dog shit out of Murder and Capone and locked them up.

CHAPTER TWENTY-THREE

"Yo, Sholomy, what's the word, man?" DeMarco asked.

"Ain't shit. Over here at my son's house."

"You must've not heard what happened."

"Nah, talk to me."

"Those soft-ass niggas from across the street called them boys on us."

"Say word!"

"Yeah, they locked up Murder and Capone and I had to take flight on them boys."

"That's crazy, that's how they playin? Yo, DeMarco, just lay low until I come out."

Sholomy came outside like two hours later and called back. "Yeah, DeMarco, where you at?"

"I'm at the low spot."

"Okay, cool, meet me in the hallway."

DeMarco opened the door, peeked out and then stepped into the hallway.

"So I'm saying, DeMarco, what you wanna do?"

"To keep it tall, I want to go over there and give them somethin to call the police for."

"Fuck it, DeMarco, I'm wit it."

They were both strapped up as Sholomy crept across the street. DeMarco went to the back door and walked quietly up the stairs.

He peeped a fiend lookin to cop. "Stacy, wassup?"

"Ain't shit, DeMarco. I was just gettin ready to walk across the street to see your boys. Your people out?"

"No, we done for the night. What you could do is take this $20, go by building four and tell me who's on the fifth floor."

"Okay, I'll be right back."

Stacy copped from them and came back to give De-Marco the scoop.

DeMarco tiptoed upstairs. As he got closer, he could hear niggas playing the song "Ten Crack Commandments."

"Yeah, pussies, don't move! First nigga even flinches gonna be the nigga headed to the hospital!"

Niggas thought they was seein a ghost.

"Y'all thought it was over?" DeMarco pulled his gun out, stripped them butt-ass naked, and threw their clothes out the window. He pistol-whipped one of the biggest niggas so bad he's still probably seeing stars. The other punks downstairs—Sholomy robbed and pistol-whipped them too.

"Damn, DeMarco, I thought it was raining. All I saw was niggas' shit flying out the window!"

"Shit, they lucky I didn't pop one of them in the head for calling the police and shit."

"Well, we got our bail money back."

"You ain't never lie."

They went right to Sholomy's grandma's house and rebagged the work to put it back on the streets.

DeMarco jumped into his car and drove to the gas station to get a calling card. He wanted to call India since he hadn't spoken to her in a while.

The phone rang four times before she picked it up.

"Hello. May I help you?"

"Yeah, this your young stallion."

"Oh, hey, baby, how you been doing? It's funny, I was just tellin your grandmother I want to come up to see you. Will you let me know, so we can make it happen?"

"So what's been goin on down there?"

"Oh, you ain't hear what happened?"

"No, put me on."

"The feds locked up your man Killer C."

"What?!"

"Yeah, baby, you left just in time. The feds locked up a lot of people down here."

"A'ight, well, I guess I'll see you when you decide to come up here."

"Okay, big man, take care of yourself."

"Okay, baby."

DeMarco hopped back into his car and started rolling up immediately. He was sick hearing about what happened to his man, knowing he could be there for the rest of his life. Pull after pull, DeMarco kept thinking about his right-hand man. His phone started ringing, it was Lefty. He paused for a moment not sure if he should answer, he gave in, "Yeah wassup?"

"Ain't shit. Just called to say we good, we still fam. Tonight I'm havin a get-together for my birthday. I want you to come through."

"Where at?"

"By my building in the park."

"Okay, cool, what time is shit gonna start?"

"Like 12."

DeMarco didn't really want to go because of the shooting incident, but decided to show his cousin some support. He called his peoples Murder and Capone, who were already back on the streets and they headed over. Bitches were all over the place and they were happy to see DeMarco. He and Sholomy had brought twenty bottles of Moët for Lefty. Niggas were getting twisted. DeMarco even took one of his old chicks between two parked cars and started fucking the shit out of her from the front, back, all kinds of crazy shit.

Afterwards, he noticed some dude across the street walking toward the park. He was saying to himself, *I have to watch these niggas*. Right then, the nigga pulled out and started shooting at everything in sight. Shit was like a movie. Niggas and bitches were shooting. DeMarco grabbed his two niggas, a bottle, and got the fuck out of there. He wasn't trying to sit around to ask any questions either.

They went back to the block where he double-parked his car.

"Y'all niggas good?"

"Hell yeah," they answered.

Capone said, "If you ask me, that shit was a setup." He sat on the curb sipping on a bottle of Moët.

DeMarco's phone rang. *Man, I ain't with it tonight. I'm going home,* he said to himself and didn't pick up. He dropped Murder and Capone off then went into his crib and called it a night.

Waking up early, DeMarco grabbed the remote off the nightstand and turned on the news.

"Last night, around 11 p.m., a shoot-out occurred at the Baisley projects in South Jamaica. One man was left dead and four others injured. At this time, there is a person of interest wanted for questioning. Police are not releasing any names yet. Once we get more information, we will have an update. Now back to you, Kim."

Damn! DeMarco thought as he replayed the night before in his head. There were too many people shooting to blame just one person.

Ring, ring.

"Who dis?"

"I know you saw the news," Capone said.

"Hell yeah, I was just watchin it."

"So, what'chu think?"

"I think I'm comin to get you. Where you at?" DeMarco asked.

"Same place you dropped me off at."

"A'ight, give me a half. I'll be there."

LaLa took the kids out, while DeMarco threw on some sweats, a t-shirt, and was out the door. Forty-five minutes later he pulled in front of the crib and blew the horn. Capone got in and they pulled off.

"So wassup, you think the boys talkin about us?" Capone asked.

"I don't know, but we gotta lay low anyway," DeMarco said. As he made the left turn off of 134th Avenue onto Farmers Boulevard, he didn't notice that a blue sedan was tailing him.

Ring, ring.

"Yo, who dis?"

"Baby, where are you?" LaLa shouted.

"I'm wit Capone, ma. Why you yelling?"

"Listen, baby, get off the streets now. The cops just left your aunt's house lookin for you, and Money told me they were showin your picture around the projects. They even went to my mom's house."

DeMarco immediately pulled over and parked behind a black truck. "A'ight, baby, I'll meet you at the house."

Unfortunately, the police were the least of DeMarco's worries. As he shifted his car into reverse, he failed to notice the shadow that loomed over him. DeMarco and Capone had both been too distracted by LaLa's phone call to notice the blue sedan that had blocked them in from behind, until it was too late. With quickness, the shadow shifted. DeMarco immediately recognized the blinding light and deafening boom for exactly what it was: payback. The smell of gunpowder hung in the air as Capone's head exploded and he slumped against the passenger's-side window.

DeMarco had no time to mourn his friend. He pulled the door handle, hopped out of his car, and instinctively reached for his waistband. The nines that usually accompanied him were not there. He turned in the direction of the shadow that held his fate in its hands.

DeMarco stared directly into the hate-filled eyes peering from behind the black mask, but he had no fear. He was Jamaica, Queens, to the bone; the hood had raised a soldier. DeMarco steeled himself for what he knew was next. Time stood still. He said a silent prayer, hoping that LaLa, Tammy, and the kids knew how much he loved them, and that they wouldn't suffer from any of the decisions he had made with his life.

DeMarco smirked, then whispered to himself, *Damn, it's true, the game don't change,* as the familiar sound of death ripped through the air toward him.